DR. MANIAC WILL
SEE YOU NOW

GOOSEBUMPS®
Also available as ebooks

NIGHT OF THE LIVING DUMMY
DEEP TROUBLE
MONSTER BLOOD
THE HAUNTED MASK
ONE DAY AT HORRORLAND
THE CURSE OF THE MUMMY'S TOMB
BE CAREFUL WHAT YOU WISH FOR
SAY CHEESE AND DIE!
THE HORROR AT CAMP JELLYJAM
HOW I GOT MY SHRUNKEN HEAD
THE WEREWOLF OF FEVER SWAMP
A NIGHT IN TERROR TOWER
WELCOME TO DEAD HOUSE
WELCOME TO CAMP NIGHTMARE
GHOST BEACH
THE SCARECROW WALKS AT MIDNIGHT
YOU CAN'T SCARE ME!
RETURN OF THE MUMMY
REVENGE OF THE LAWN GNOMES
PHANTOM OF THE AUDITORIUM
VAMPIRE BREATH
STAY OUT OF THE BASEMENT
A SHOCKER ON SHOCK STREET
LET'S GET INVISIBLE!
NIGHT OF THE LIVING DUMMY 2
NIGHT OF THE LIVING DUMMY 3
THE ABOMINABLE SNOWMAN OF PASADENA
THE BLOB THAT ATE EVERYONE
THE GHOST NEXT DOOR
THE HAUNTED CAR
ATTACK OF THE GRAVEYARD GHOULS
PLEASE DON'T FEED THE VAMPIRE

ALSO AVAILABLE:
IT CAME FROM OHIO!: MY LIFE AS A WRITER by R.L. Stine

Goosebumps®

MOST WANTED

DR. MANIAC WILL SEE YOU NOW

R.L. STINE

SCHOLASTIC INC.

ISBN 978-0-545-41802-7

12 11 10 9 8 7 6   14 15 16 17 18/0

Printed in the U.S.A.   40
First printing, October 2013

WELCOME. YOU ARE MOST WANTED.

Hello. Come in. Don't stand on the WELCOME mat. It's sleeping, and it gets angry when people wake it up.

Actually, I don't think it's a WELCOME mat at all. I think it's a very furry stingray that crawled to shore. Go ahead. Step on it. See what it does.

OUCH. You woke him up — didn't you? Ooh, that's a nasty sting. Why don't you scream a lot and see if that helps get rid of the pain?

While you're screaming, come on inside. Welcome to the Goosebumps office. I'm R.L. Stine. This is where I write all the books.

Just shove those drooling Gila monsters out of your way. I really should have this place cleaned.

No. Don't sit there. That's not a chair. It's my grandfather. I'll dust him off so you can see him better. Look. I think he's smiling. Cute.

I see you're admiring the WANTED posters on the wall. Those posters show the creepiest,

1

crawliest, grossest villains of all time. They are the MOST WANTED bad guys from the MOST WANTED Goosebumps books.

That crazy-looking dude in the weird costume with the leopard-skin cape and the yellow-feathered boots? Of *course* he's on a WANTED poster. DR. MANIAC is the Most Wanted Maniac on the planet.

What is so evil about him? A boy named Richard Dreezer will tell you the whole story. It's pretty scary — especially when Richard found himself *at the end of the world!*

Go ahead. Start the story — if you dare. *Dr. Maniac Will See You Now!*

Hold on. I can't start my story yet. I have to sneeze.

CHOOOOOOOOOO.

Yes, I sneeze a lot. I can't help it. I have a lot of allergies.

My name is Richard Dreezer, but the kids at my school call me Richard *Sneezer*. Funny, huh?

Some kids call me the Faucet because my nose runs all the time. That's not funny, either.

Having a lot of allergies is a riot — *only* to people who don't have a lot of allergies.

I wish that was my only problem. I am also the only kid in the sixth grade with red hair and a face full of freckles. And I'm short and thin and look about eight even though I'm twelve. What can I do about that? Nothing.

Maybe this is why I daydream a lot. I mean, a *lot*. And maybe this is why comic books are so important to me. I mean, I like to imagine I'm this big, hulking, powerful superhero-guy, with wavy black hair and rippling muscles. And I can fly and escape to a new world any time I want.

Sometimes I sit in class and daydream about being *evil*. I call myself the Revenger. And I use my incredible powers to take my revenge on the kids who sneeze at me and mess up my red hair and call me names.

I defeat them all and leave them collapsed in a heap on the classroom floor. And then I take Bree Birnbaum's hand, and the two of us fly out the window and sail over the town. And we fly to my secret Fortress of Coolness, the source of my amazing powers and my true home.

Yes, I have a crush on Bree Birnbaum. Everyone at Hugh Jackman Middle School knows it. Everyone but Bree, that is.

Today I was daydreaming about my Fortress of Coolness. I keep the Crystals of Many Colors there, and I needed them fast. Each crystal holds a power. I ran through the secret tunnel to the underground vault where they're hidden. When I reached them, I quickly wrapped my hand around the red crystal —

Whoa. Did someone just call my name?

"Richard? Earth calling Richard Dreezer? Can you hear me?"

Oh, wow. It was Mrs. Callus, my teacher. I guess she had been calling my name for a while. Everyone in the room was staring at me.

I leaned forward on my desk and raised my eyes to her. "Yes?"

Mrs. Callus squinted at me. "Richard? Where were you? Were you on Planet Dreezer again?"

Everyone laughed.

Actually, Mrs. Callus is very nice. She's young and very cool looking. She doesn't look old enough to be a teacher. She has short blond hair and a great smile and a diamond stud in her nose. And she wears jeans and rock band T-shirts to school.

"Richard, are you ready to give your book report?" she asked.

A stab of fear ran down my body. I *hate* getting up in front of the class. I think I'm allergic to it. I felt a big sneeze coming on. I held my breath to fight it back.

"Y-yes," I stammered.

"What book did you read?" she asked.

"Actually, it was a graphic novel," I said. "It's about the zombie apocalypse, but the zombies are the good guys. It's called *War of the Zombie Freakazoids.*"

She motioned toward the front of the room. "Come up here and tell us about it."

My chair made a loud scraping sound as I climbed to my feet. I picked up my two-page book report and started to carry it down the aisle. My hands were suddenly cold and sweaty.

"Mrs. Callus, are we allowed to read comic books for our report?"

That was Marcus Maloney. He's a pain. He's always on my case. He's always on everyone's case.

Why is he so mean? Maybe because he's the *biggest sixth grader in the world*? He's a little bit bigger than a whale I saw last summer at SeaWorld. Know what he likes to do? He likes to walk up to you and bump you down the hall with his stomach.

"It — it's not a comic book," I said. "It's a graphic novel."

I was almost to the front of the room when my sneeze exploded.

CHOOOOOOOOOO-EEEY.

I sneezed all over Lateesha Franklin, who sits in the front row. I couldn't help it. I couldn't turn away in time. I told you, my sneezes are majorly big.

She screamed and waved her arms in the air. Like she was trying to shield herself.

Too late.

Then she went crazy, wiping off her sweater with both hands. I saw that I totally sprayed her from head to foot.

"Sorry," I muttered.

I don't know if she heard me. The others were laughing so loud. Marcus Maloney laughed so loud, he fell off his chair. Nice.

Whoa. I turned my head and sneezed again. A big glob of snot splattered the chalkboard.

6

Now everyone was in hysterics. I mean, ha-ha. How funny was it?

"People. People . . ." Mrs. Callus jumped to her feet and struggled to quiet everyone. "We've talked about this before. It's not nice to make fun of someone who is allergic —"

That's when I let go with my loudest, wettest sneeze yet.

Oh, noooo.

I totally sprayed Mrs. Callus. It was like a tsunami of snot.

She groaned and spun away. Her hands stabbed at the sides of her T-shirt. I could see glistening wet stuff in her hair.

"S-sorry . . ." I murmured.

When she turned back to me, her expression had changed. Her eyes were wide — with *fury*. She uttered an angry groan. "Richard —" Her voice was ugly, menacing.

I took a step back. *What is she going to do?*

She lurched toward me. And with superhuman strength, she lifted me off the floor . . . swung me high in the air . . . and *heaved* me through the plate glass window.

No. That didn't happen. That was a daydream. I imagined it.

Maybe I *do* read too many comic books.

Mrs. Callus didn't heave me out the third-floor window. She just told me to forget about my report till later. And she sent me back to my seat.

That was *worse* than sailing out the window. Because I had to listen to everyone laughing at me and making fun of me. I lowered my head and stared straight ahead and tried to force their ugly voices from my ears.

How totally embarrassing.

I could feel my nose running. I wiped it with the sleeve of my shirt. I tossed my book report onto my desk and dropped into my seat.

Mrs. Callus was still wiping off her T-shirt with a handkerchief. I knew I hadn't heard the end of this. I knew that drowning the teacher in snot would haunt me all day.

And I was right.

After school, Marcus Maloney and a bunch of other kids followed me down the hall, sneezing their heads off. They thought they were hilarious. All sneezing together as loud as they could and hee-hawing like donkeys.

They won't be laughing when the Revenger has his way.

That's what I was thinking when I saw Bree Birnbaum at the back of the group. She was laughing, too.

That was cold. That really hurt.

They followed me outside, giggling and sneezing on me. Marcus Maloney bumped me from behind and sent me sailing headfirst over the hedge at the bottom of the school yard.

I hit the ground hard on my stomach. My backpack bounced on top of me.

When I looked up, I saw my parents' yellow Camry parked across the street. I pulled myself to my feet, stumbled away from the laughing kids, and jerked open the back door of the car.

Dad sat behind the wheel. Mom turned and smiled at me. "Hi, Richard. Looks like you were having fun with your friends."

"Yeah. Fun," I muttered.

She's totally clueless. No point in telling her the truth.

Dad had his eyes on his phone. He mumbled something under his breath. It sounded like, "Mumble mumble." Dad is a great mumbler.

My parents are, like, out of a horror movie. They are both incredibly thin and pale as zombies. Dad grumbles and groans like the Frankenstein monster. When Mom smiles, her teeth shoot out like fangs.

Okay. Maybe I exaggerate.

But Mom only smiles for my little brother, Ernie. He's a spoiled monster, but she thinks everything he does is adorable.

Also, my parents spend most of their time arguing. They argue about everything. It's like it's their hobby.

How did I get in this family? Seriously.

I'm pretty sure I'm a superhero alien from another planet. I came to Earth as a baby, and these people, the Dreezers, adopted me.

It's the only good explanation I can think of.

I settled back in the seat. "Why are you picking me up?" I asked.

Dad pulled the car away from the curb. "Ask your mother," he mumbled.

"I saw an ad for an allergy doctor," Mom said.

"You're taking me to a new doctor?"

"He might be able to help you," Mom replied.

"He doesn't need an allergy doctor," Dad said, turning onto Kirby Street.

"Yes, he does," Mom snapped. "Be quiet, Barry."

"Don't tell me to be quiet. He doesn't need a doctor. He needs to man up."

"You can't blame Richard if he has bad allergies," Mom said.

"Bad allergies? He has a bad *attitude*, that's all."

They started to shout at each other. I pressed my hands over my ears. Mom and Dad fight like this all the time. I should be used to it.

If I were going to draw a comic book about my family, I'd call it *Battle Quest: Attack of the Screaming Parents*.

Sometimes Ernie and I hide at the top of the stairs and listen to them argue. We make funny faces and jokes, and try not to let them hear us crack up.

But it's not funny when they fight about *me*. That's what I really hate.

And now here they were screaming at each other about whether I needed an allergy doctor or not.

"I can't keep the kid in tissues," Dad grumbled. "He goes through a box a day."

"What? Do you want him to reuse them?" Mom shouted. "Maybe give him a tissue a day? Would that save you money, Barry?"

I felt a really big sneeze coming on.

Luckily, it was a short drive. Dad turned onto Ditko Avenue, went a few blocks, then pulled the car to the curb.

I gazed out the window and saw a dark brick building. A small sign next to a glass door read: DR. ROOT, ALLERGIST AND REALLY GOOD DOCTOR.

"Whoa!" I let out a cry. "Look where we are! Right across the street from the Comic Book Museum."

Yes! How lucky was this?

The Comic Book Museum is where I spend all my spare time. I know every inch of the place. I wish I could *live* there. They have the biggest, most amazing collection of comic books in the world. No. Maybe the universe.

"Dr. Root is expecting you," Mom said. "Be sure to tell him about how your skin itches when you eat tortilla chips."

"Aren't you coming in with me?" I asked.

"We can't," Dad said. "We have to pick up Ernie."

"Where's Ernie?" I asked.

"At his pottery class," Mom answered. She gets a special smile on her face when she talks about her precious Ernie.

"He doesn't make pottery," I said. "He just throws clay at the other kids."

Truth.

"Don't say bad things about Ernie," Mom snapped.

"At least Ernie doesn't sneeze his brains out every five minutes and drip snot all over the carpet," Dad added.

Nice.

See, Ernie can't do anything wrong. Seriously.

They think everything my kid brother does is adorable.

I climbed out of the car. The cool afternoon breeze felt good on my face. The sun was beginning to drop behind the downtown buildings. Long purple shadows stretched across the sidewalk.

I glanced across the street at the big, white stone museum with its domed roof. *I'll stop by there after my doctor appointment,* I decided.

"See you later," I called to my parents. I slammed the car door shut. They were already arguing about something else.

I turned and stepped up to the glass door. I glanced at the doctor's sign again. Then I pulled the door open and stepped into the building.

How was I to know that the whole world was about to go crazy?

A sign in the lobby told me Dr. Root was in Room 301. I took an elevator to the third floor and found the office at the end of a long, dimly lit hallway.

I stepped into a pale green waiting room. No one there. No one seated at the reception desk at the front. I saw two pale green couches against the wall. A low table was stacked with a pile of old *People* magazines.

"Anyone here?" I called.

No answer.

"Dr. Root?" My voice rang loudly through the empty office.

I was about to leave when I heard footsteps from a back room. Heavy, thudding footsteps. The back office door opened, and a huge man in a white short-sleeved lab coat lumbered out.

He had short black hair over a round red face that looked like an inflated balloon. His enormous belly pushed against the front of the lab

14

coat. I could see that two or three buttons had popped off. Fat folds of his stomach poked out. His arms were bare and pink, like two big hams.

He had tiny, black bird eyes tucked into his head. And when he smiled at me, folds of fat formed three or four chins under his mouth.

"I ... I think I'm in the wrong office," I stammered.

His smile spread. "No. I've been expecting you, Richard." His voice was soft and seemed to come from deep inside him.

His body bounced as he stepped toward me. He reached out a pink hand to shake. His fingers looked like fat sausages. Standing so close, I could see big drops of sweat on his forehead.

He held on to my hand. His hand was warm and spongy. His tiny eyes locked on me. "I hear you have allergy problems," he said. "You sneeze a lot, yes?"

"Yes," I said. My voice cracked. I cleared my throat.

He finally let go of my hand. He nodded, studying me. Out the window, I could see the Comic Book Museum across the street. I really wanted to be there instead of in this empty office with this weirdo blob of a doctor bulging out of his lab coat.

I mean, he was like Marcus Maloney gone WILD.

"Don't be nervous, Richard," he said softly. "I think I can help you. I have my own treatment.

It's taken me years to develop. But I think I can change your life."

"Uh . . . change my life?"

"Follow me." He turned and waddled to the back office.

I tried to hold it in, but I couldn't. I sneezed. And then sneezed again.

"I believe you are allergic to dust in the air," Dr. Root said. "You are very sensitive. You are allergic to tiny particles."

I wiped my nose with my shirt sleeve. I stepped into the back room. It was also green. Green wallpaper. Green countertops. Even the light seemed to be green.

He was bent over a cabinet drawer. The flab on his arms rippled as he searched through the drawer. "Would you like to stop all the sneezing, Richard?"

"Well, yes. I sure would," I said. "But I've had these allergies since I was born. I —"

"I'm going to give you one shot," he said. He stood up. I couldn't see what he held in his hand. It was hidden behind the bulging lab coat.

A stab of fear shot down my back. "One shot?"

He nodded. "Yes. I think that's all it will take. One shot, and your allergies will disappear." He motioned for me to turn around. "I'm going to give you the shot in your back."

My mouth suddenly felt dry. I'm not good with shots. I've had a lot of allergy shots. And I wasn't

16

brave about any of them. "I don't know if —" I started.

"Don't move, Richard," he said. "It will only pinch for a few seconds. But don't move. Please. Don't turn around."

I held my breath. I tightened all my muscles. I shut my eyes and waited for the stab of pain in my back.

One . . . two . . . three . . .

I counted silently to myself. Waiting . . . waiting for the pinch of pain.

. . . four . . . five . . .

I couldn't take it. I opened my eyes and looked behind me.

And saw the needle raised in Dr. Root's hand. It was *two feet long*!

Before I could move, he pressed it into my back.

I uttered a hoarse scream.

Everything went black.

I opened my eyes. I blinked a few times, then stared up at a pale green sky.

Sky?

Where am I?

No. I saw a long ceiling light. The ceiling was green. I raised my head. Blinked some more. Dr. Root's office slowly came into focus.

I cleared my throat. Took a few breaths. It took me a while to realize I was flat on my back.

Dr. Root leaned over me. His face was as red as a tomato. His tiny black eyes gazed down at me. "Sorry, Richard," he said in a whisper.

"Am I — ?" The ceiling spun in circles above me.

"You're okay," he said, patting my arm. "You fainted. I'm afraid you're not the first person to faint because of that long needle." He shook his head. "I told you not to look."

"I . . . I couldn't help it. I —"

He grabbed my shoulders gently and pulled me up to a sitting position. "You'll be okay now," he said. "That shot looks terrifying, but you'll see. It really will help you."

My dizziness faded. I started to feel better. I climbed to my feet.

Dr. Root wiped sweat off his cheeks with both hands. He smiled again, his chins folding like pie dough beneath his mouth. "It didn't hurt, did it?"

"I . . . I guess not," I stammered. "I mean, I didn't feel anything."

"Good," he said softly. "I'm glad." He motioned to the front. "You can go now. I don't think you'll need another shot. But if you need me, I'm easy to find."

"Well . . . thank you," I said.

Awkward. I just wanted to get out of there.

I turned and walked to the waiting room. He didn't follow me. I stepped out into the hall, strode quickly to the elevator, and took it down to the ground floor.

I stepped outside. The afternoon sun was low in the sky. The breeze had grown cooler. I raised my eyes to the museum. I couldn't wait to get over there.

I looked for traffic. Started to jog across the street. And . . .

CHOOOOOOO-EEEEY.

5

I stepped into the wide front entryway to the museum. The ceiling was a mile high, lined with tall windows. A huge red-and-blue chandelier hung down over the long front desk.

My shoes clicked on the white marble floor. The sound echoed through the enormous room. My eyes swept over the big posters of super-heroes that covered the walls.

"Hey, Kahuna. How's it going?" I shouted.

Behind the desk, Kahuna looked up from the graphic novel he was reading. "Yo, Richard. Keeping it real?"

Big Kahuna is the main greeter and curator of the museum. I don't know his real name. I call him Kahuna. We're like friends. I mean, I spend more time with him than with my own family.

Kahuna has a long, serious face. He wears black-framed glasses. He has dark brown hair pulled back in a ponytail. Dangling from one ear, he has a big silver pirate hoop earring. And he has colorful tattoos of his favorite superheroes up and down his arms and across his chest. He wears sleeveless T-shirts to show them off.

He's a cool guy, but I've never seen him smile.

I stepped up to the desk. "Shazam, bro," he said. We bumped knuckles. "Where have you been lately?"

I spun around and sneezed. I held my breath and made sure I wasn't going to sneeze again. Then I turned back to him. "Just been to the allergy doctor," I said. "He gave me a shot."

Kahuna snickered. "I don't think it's working." He pulled open a drawer under the desk and reached inside. "Got something for you."

He pulled out two comic books. I couldn't see the covers, but they looked pretty old. The paper was yellow.

Kahuna is the greatest dude ever. He always finds comics he knows I'll like. And he pretty much lets me do whatever I want in the museum. I can go into any of the rare comics rooms and spend as much time as I want looking at the old collections.

He raised the comics for me to see. On the covers, I saw a chimpanzee with a black mask pulled down over his head. "The Masked Monkey!" I cried.

Kahuna nodded. "These are very rare, bro. The only two Masked Monkey comics ever produced. From 1973. You seen them before? *Of course* you haven't." He answered his own question.

My hands shook a little as I took the two comics from him. These were very rare and valuable. "Awesome," I said. "Totally awesome. I'll take them to the reading room and read them. Thanks, Kahuna."

We bumped knuckles again. Then I carefully gripped the comics in front of me as I made my way to the reading room at the back of the long front hall.

My shoes clicked on the marble floor. I hurried past the bronze statues of the Martian Mayhem and his archenemy, Plutopus.

Some days I stopped to look at the hundreds of framed comic book covers that spread over one entire wall. But not today. I was too eager to study these valuable Masked Monkey comics.

I didn't see anyone else in the museum. Why wasn't it more popular? Didn't people realize this was the best comic book museum in the *world*?

I passed the video projection room and the tall statue of Captain Protoplasm. The auditorium stood dark and silent.

I trotted to the end of the hall. I knew I didn't have much time. My parents were probably at home now, arguing over what we should have for dinner.

"Oh, wow." I let out a cry when I saw that the reading room doors were closed. I grabbed the knob and turned it. "No. Please."

The doors were locked.

I turned and started back to the front to get the key from Kahuna. As I walked, I carefully wiped my hands on the legs of my jeans. I didn't want to get sweat on the valuable comics.

I was halfway to the front desk when I heard shouts. I heard a crash. Then a dull THUD. Another shout.

Was Kahuna fighting with someone?

I took off, running to the desk. My shoes skidded on the slick floor. My heart started to pound.

The desk came into view. But — whoa. Where was Kahuna?

He wasn't in his usual place, sitting on the tall stool behind the desk.

I skidded to a stop. I stared at the stranger behind the desk. I couldn't see his face. He had his back turned.

I tucked the Masked Monkey comics into my backpack and stepped up to the desk. "Hey, where's Kahuna?" I asked. My voice came out high and shrill.

"He had to leave," the man replied. He didn't turn around.

I blinked. Something was weird. The man was standing in the tall trash can behind the desk.

I stared at his back. He wore a long black trench coat. He had silver hair falling down over the collar.

Slowly, he turned to face me — and I let out a startled gasp.

His eyes — they had no pupils. No color in them at all. They were solid white.

"Can I help you?" he asked.

I stared into those blank white eyes. No pupils. No irises. None at all. Was he blind?

"Can I help you?" he repeated. His voice was scratchy and hoarse. His head was bald and shiny and shaped like a light bulb.

"Uh . . . no," I said. "I mean . . ."

He picked up a pencil and scribbled some words on the desk pad.

He's not blind. But he has no pupils.

"I'm . . . uh . . . late for dinner," I stammered. "I'll come back when Kahuna is here."

He nodded. "Have a *super* evening," he said. But he said it coldly. Like a threat.

A chill of fear made me shudder. What was this about? I knew I'd heard a shout and then a crash. And then suddenly, this weird dude stood behind Kahuna's desk.

"Bye," I said. I spun away from the desk and ran out of the museum.

* * *

I didn't realize I'd taken the Masked Monkey comics home with me until after dinner.

We had a typical dinner at the Dreezer house. Mom and Dad argued about whether the short ribs were tender enough. Ernie was clowning around and acting like a jerk, pretending he was a string puppet. And he spilled his apple juice. But of course they didn't shout at him or anything because everything he does is adorable.

I dropped a carrot on the floor, and Mom and Dad started shouting about what a clumsy klutz I am. Then I sneezed on my dinner plate, and they told me to leave the table.

Typical.

Up in my room, I started to unload my backpack — and there they were. The two rare comic books.

I knew I had to return them to the museum tomorrow. Kahuna would understand that I didn't mean to take them.

I carefully spread the comics on my desk and began to read the first one.

Even though the hero was a monkey, the art was very realistic. The intro said that no one knew the origin of the Masked Monkey. His power is in his mask. He may be as small as a chimp, but he has the strength of *ten gorillas*.

"That's a mean monkey!" I murmured to myself.

Downstairs, I heard my parents arguing over the best way to load the dishwasher. And then I heard another, closer sound. The THUD of running footsteps.

I spun around as Ernie came bursting into my room. He let out a cry and ran straight to my desk.

"Stop!" I cried. I tried to shove him away.

Too late. He grabbed the two comics and took off with them.

The little thief is always taking my things. But this time he'd gone too far.

I jumped to my feet. "Give those back!" I shouted. "Now! I'm not going to play around with you!"

He stopped in the hall and stuck his tongue out at me.

I took a few steps toward him. I kept my eyes on the comics. I was trembling, so angry I thought I could explode.

"Those are valuable," I said. "They belong to the museum. They are very rare. Give them back to me."

Ernie shook his head. He had a sick grin on his weasel face. "They're mine now," he said.

"GIVE THEM BACK!" I shrieked.

Mom stuck her head into the doorway. "What's all the racket?"

"Ernie stole my comic books," I said breathlessly. "They're not mine. They belong to the museum. He stole them. Make him give them back. Make him. Make him!"

Mom glanced at Ernie. Ernie pressed the comics to his chest.

"Calm down, Richard," Mom said. "Why are you being so mean to your brother?"

"HUH?" I cried. "*Me*? Being mean to *him*?"

Mom smiled at Ernie. "Richard, don't you see how cute that is? Ernie wants to be just like *you*. That's so sweet."

"But — but — but —" I sputtered. "I — I can't believe you're taking his side. Why do you always take his side?"

"I'm not taking sides," Mom said. "I just think you should stop picking on your little brother."

Ernie stuck his tongue out at me again. Then he tossed the comic books into my room.

I wanted to scream. I wanted to scream and rip something to pieces. Anything.

I waited till Mom and Ernie went downstairs. Then I opened my mouth wide to utter an angry cry. But I sneezed instead. I sneezed three or four times.

The allergy shot was worthless. "Dr. Root is a quack," I muttered.

I wiped my nose with my sleeve. I carefully placed the comic books back on my desk.

My anger faded. I suddenly felt sad. Sad and lonely.

I wish I had the strength of ten gorillas, I thought.

The characters in comic books have such

exciting lives. They have all kinds of action and thrills all day and night. People don't laugh at them because they have allergies. They have good friends who come to their rescue when they're in danger.

It's no wonder I daydream about superheroes and comic books. If you had my life, you'd daydream, too.

"I'm the Masked Monkey!" I suddenly shouted. I pictured myself covered in fur, big, powerful, rippling muscles, a black mask over my head to protect my identity.

"I have the strength of ten gorillas!"

I began running around my room, thumping my chest with both fists. I howled and bellowed and made furious gorilla groans and cries. I leaped onto my bed. Jumped up and down, beating my chest and howling.

And then my breath caught in my throat. I gasped. My eyes bulged. I froze there on the bed — and stared at Bree Birnbaum, watching me from the doorway.

My knees wobbled. I almost fell off the bed.

Bree tossed her blond hair behind her shoulder. She tilted her head and squinted at me. "Richard? What are you *doing*?" she demanded.

"Uh..."

What could I say? No way I could tell her I was the Masked Monkey with the strength of ten gorillas.

"Well...it's a special exercise," I said. "It's supposed to help me get rid of my allergies."

I couldn't tell if she believed me or not. She just kept squinting at me with those clear, beautiful green eyes.

She wore a green sweater that matched her eyes, and a short pleated skirt over dark jeans.

I jumped off the bed. I brushed back my hair with one hand. My face was sweaty. Being a gorilla was hard work.

Bree stepped into the room and glanced

around. She studied the Mamba Mama poster over my bed. "Ooh, sick," she said. "That woman is part snake?"

"Well, she's a teacher in a nursery school. But she can transform into a deadly, venomous snake when she wants to," I explained.

Bree rolled her eyes. "Whatever."

I sat down on the edge of my bed. "What are you doing here?" I asked.

She rolled her eyes again. "Good question. I guess it's just my lucky day."

Bree is very sarcastic. I'm kind of used to it. We've been in the same class since kindergarten. I think I had a crush on her when we were five. Even after she dumped the class ant farm on my head.

She plopped down on my desk chair. "Richard, you know Mrs. Callus teamed partners up for museum projects," she said.

"She did?"

"You have to stop daydreaming in class, Richard. She did — and you're my museum partner. I was the lucky one to get you."

"Cool," I said.

I knew she was being sarcastic again. But so what? Bree and I working on a project together? How awesome was that?

"So, I guess we have to do this project together," she said. "But you have to promise me one thing."

"What is it?" I asked.

"You have to promise you won't tell anyone we're working together."

I thought about it for a few seconds. "Okay."

"Raise your right hand and swear."

I raised my right hand and swore. "I won't tell anyone we're working together."

"Okay." She settled back on the chair. She picked up the little statue of my favorite comic villain, the Scab. She rolled it around in her hand. "Oh, sick. Why is it so scratchy?"

"He has a lot of scabs," I said. "Be careful with that. It was a birthday present."

She squinted at me. "You're not normal, are you?"

That made me laugh.

"I'm not joking," she said. She set the Scab down next to my autographed photo of the Caped Wolf. Then she jumped to her feet. "I have to get out of here. This room is making me nauseous."

"Does that mean you don't want to do our project in the Comic Book Museum?" I asked.

She stuck her finger down her throat and made a barfing sound. I guessed that meant no.

I followed her to the door. "Bree, do you want to get an A?"

"Of course."

"Then we'll do the Comic Book Museum," I said. "I know everything about it. Every corner. Every display. Every everything."

"So?"

"So, I'll do all the work. I'll do the whole project. It will be fun for me. And I promise we'll get an A."

She crossed her arms in front of her and squinted at me for a long time. "You'll do all the work?"

I raised my right hand again. "I swear."

She thought about it a while. Then she tossed back her blond hair. "Okay, I guess."

"Awesome," I said. "So you'll take the bus with me to the museum after school tomorrow?"

"No. I'll meet you there. I don't want anyone from school seeing us together." She spun away and hurried down the stairs.

This is going to work out great! I thought.

The next morning, my head felt like a water balloon. And I was a total snot machine. I sneezed so hard, I thought I would blow my head off. And my eyes were running so badly, I could barely see.

I started to brush my teeth and sneezed all over the bathroom mirror. I tried to wipe my eyes with a towel, but they kept running like the water fountain at school that you can't turn off.

I pulled on some clothes and went down to breakfast. Mom and Dad were already arguing, something about whether it was a windy day or not.

I sat down in my place across from Ernie. He had oatmeal smeared all over his chin. He opened his mouth wide, showing me the mushed-up oatmeal inside.

Is he gross enough?

I picked up the Pop-Tart on my plate and took a bite of it. My favorite. Cherry.

"We're supposed to have thirty-mile-per-hour winds," Dad said.

"You call that wind? Barry, that's no wind at all," Mom replied.

"I didn't say it was a hurricane," Dad snapped. "Why don't you ever listen to me?"

"Why don't you ever say anything worth listening to?"

Ernie grabbed the Pop-Tart off my plate and shoved it into his mouth.

"Hey — that's mine!" I cried. I grabbed for it. But he giggled and swung his head away from my grasp, chewing furiously.

"Mom? Dad? Ernie stole my Pop-Tart!" I shouted.

They both turned to Ernie. "It's cherry," Mom said. "That's Ernie's favorite."

"But — but —" I sputtered.

"He was just being funny," Mom said, smiling at him. "Let him have it, Richard."

"You eat too many sweets," Dad said to me. "Why don't you go get a grapefruit from the fridge."

"Huh? A grapefruit?"

Mom poked Dad on the chest. "Are you saying I don't give him a healthy breakfast? Are you saying I don't feed the kids right?"

I tuned them out. I only wanted to think about after school today. Bree and me meeting at the

Comic Book Museum. I couldn't wait to show it off to her.

I blew my nose three or four times and wiped my runny eyes. Then I pulled on my jacket and flung my backpack over my shoulder. I walk Ernie to school every morning. And every morning he thinks it's a riot to jump on my back and shout, "Piggyback! Piggyback!"

It's not funny. This morning, he leaped onto my back and sent me crashing headfirst into the wall.

A few minutes later, we crossed Orlando Street and turned onto Kubert. It was a cool autumn day. Red and yellow leaves rained down from the trees as the wind swirled around.

I zipped my jacket to the top. "Whoa. Wait." I grabbed Ernie by the shoulder.

Was I seeing things?

I blinked my runny eyes, struggling to clear them. *Yes!* I saw two figures scampering across the red roof of the Romita family's house across the street.

But — but —

"No way!" I gasped.

They were both bent over as they darted across the roof. Both dressed from head to foot in green.

I wiped my eyes and stared hard. *This is impossible. It can't be!*

I was staring at the Frog Mutant — Captain Croaker. And he was followed by his little sidekick, Terry Tadpole.

"Hey — is that *you*?" I shouted up at them.

I was staring into the sun. I couldn't see clearly at all. They disappeared to the other side of the roof.

My heart was pounding. My brain spun.

I grabbed Ernie by the shoulders. "Did you see them?" I cried. "Did you see it, too?"

He nodded. "Yeah. I saw it."

"You did?" I shouted, still gripping his shoulders. "I'm not crazy? You saw it, too?"

"Yeah. I saw that red car go by," Ernie said. "The one with the dog hanging out the window."

"Huh?" I let go of him and staggered back. "You — you didn't see those two guys on the roof? The guys in green costumes?"

He shook his head. "I didn't see anyone on a roof."

How could he see them? They're not real.

I stood there, in a daze. I stared at the roof. Empty now. A bird landed on the chimney. It fluttered its wings and settled down, like it owned the house.

I let out a cry as Ernie stomped on my foot as hard as he could. "You little creep!" I screamed. "Why'd you do that?"

He shrugged. "Just felt like it, I guess."

I limped the rest of the way to his school. I thought maybe the little brat broke a hundred bones in my foot. But I wasn't thinking about the pain. I was thinking about Captain Croaker and Terry Tadpole.

I saw them so clearly. It *had* to be them.

But how could it be?

I felt totally confused. I thought about it all day.

After school, I looked for Bree. Maybe she had changed her mind — maybe she wanted to take the bus with me to the Comic Book Museum. But I didn't see her anywhere.

I sat in the back of the bus as it bounced into town. I couldn't wait to tell Kahuna what I saw on the Romita family's roof. I was sure he'd believe me. And I knew he'd have ideas about why I saw them. Like maybe there's a comic book costume contest in town.

I ran up the steep concrete steps and burst through the double glass doors. Then I flew across the main hall to the welcome desk. "Kahuna!" I started.

Whoa. He wasn't there.

Instead, a tall masked man, dressed in a tight costume of green and yellow, stared back at me from the other side of the desk. Two curled white fangs on his mask moved as he leaned toward me.

Once I got over my surprise, I recognized him. The SnakeMan from Saturn. "Why are you here, sssssonny?" he hissed.

"Uh . . . I'm . . . uh . . ." I took a breath. "That's an awesome costume," I said. "Did you make it?"

He didn't answer. The fangs appeared to curl tighter on the sides of his mask. His face was covered except for his eyes and mouth. He opened his lips, and a black forked tongue flicked out.

Oh, wow. How does he do that? He's a total freak!

"Where is Big Kahuna?" I asked.

"Who issss he?" he asked. The split tongue darted from side to side, then disappeared back into his mouth.

"He . . . he works here in the afternoon," I stammered. That tongue was too *weird*.

The costumed man brought his face close to mine. His eyes were green-yellow. "I don't think sssso," he said.

He was definitely creeping me out. I turned to the front doors to see if Bree had arrived. No. Not yet.

"My friend and I are doing a project about this museum," I said. "You know. A school project."

The masked man shook his head. "No. You're not," he rasped. Through the mask, the weird yellow-green eyes burned into mine.

A chill ran down my back. I retreated a few steps. "I . . . don't understand," I stammered.

"You have to leave," he said. "This museum is closed."

10

I took another step back, away from the desk —
and realized the man was standing in the
wastebasket. He made a hissing snake sound as
he stepped out of it.

He slithered out from behind the desk. The
white fangs on his mask glowed under the bright
ceiling lights. His green-yellow eyes narrowed.

"We're clossssssed," he hissed. "Go away. Go
do your project at another museum."

What was going *on* here? How could this be
happening?

I was so startled and confused, I froze.

He moved quickly. He stepped up to me. His
eyes were terrifying. His mouth opened again,
revealing the black forked tongue.

"Please —" I uttered. "Don't hurt me.
Don't —" My breath caught in my throat.

To my shock, he stepped past me. His eyes were
on the front doors now. He raised a yellow-gloved

hand and pulled a long strand of web from the shoulder of his costume.

Frozen to the floor, I watched him pull the web — like a slender rope — from his shoulder. Ignoring me completely, he walked to the doors. He pushed them open. Then he flung the long strand of rope into the air — and leaped onto it!

The rope rose high, carrying him into the air. Through the glass doors, I could see him cross the street standing stiffly on the flying rope, higher ... higher ... until he vanished from view.

Whoa.

I suddenly realized I'd stopped breathing at least a minute ago. I let out my breath in a long whoosh. Then I sank to my knees on the marble floor.

I was stunned. In shock. *I must be insanely insane*, I thought.

"What just happened?" I muttered to myself. I rubbed my eyes. I gazed around the empty museum. "I didn't see that. I didn't see the SnakeMan from Saturn sail out of here on his Wonder Web."

I stayed down on my knees, struggling to catch my breath. I pictured him slithering out of the wastebasket, his fangs curling on the sides of his mask. Moving toward me ... hissing at me ...

"The museum is closed," he said.

But how could that be?

Where was Kahuna? Where was anyone else?

I opened my mouth in a loud sneeze. Like an explosion, it echoed off the high walls. I sneezed again. I couldn't stop it.

I was still sneezing, still on my knees, when the museum doors opened.

I turned to the doors — and let out a scream.

"What are *you* doing here?"

11

Ernie bounced into the front hall. He crossed his eyes and stuck his tongue out at me.

"What are you doing here?" I repeated.

Then I saw Bree walk in behind him. She shook her head hard, tossing her hair behind her shoulder. "I brought you a surprise," she said. "Him!"

"I don't understand," I said. "Why — ?"

"Why are you on your knees on the floor?" Bree demanded.

"Oh." I climbed quickly to my feet. "I . . . uh . . . dropped a bus token," I lied.

"Your mom stopped me on the way to the museum," she said. "She dropped him with me. She said we have to watch the little monster."

Ernie let out a loud roar. He likes being called a monster. He thinks it's a compliment.

Bree bent down to rub her shin. "Will you tell him to please stop pinching my leg?"

"Ernie, stop pinching Bree's leg," I said.

He roared again. "I'm a monster. I have to pinch." He burst out laughing. He really cracks himself up. Then Ernie took off, running down the long hall, his arms stretched out like he was flying, roaring at the top of his lungs.

"We've got bigger problems than Ernie," I told Bree.

She lowered her backpack to the floor and unzipped her jacket. She gazed around. "Hey, Richard, where *is* everyone?"

"Something strange is going on," I said. "A guy told me the museum is closed."

She picked up her backpack. "Okay. Let's go."

"No! Wait!" I cried. "I'm not sure what's happening. I mean —"

I suddenly realized I didn't see Ernie. "Hey — Ernie!" I shouted. "Ernie! Where are you?"

The kid loves to wander off and make everyone look for him. Dad refuses to take him to the mall because he always gets lost. On purpose.

Mom thinks that's cute. She calls him *My Little Explorer.*

Bree and I both stared down the long front hall. "Do you see him anywhere?" I asked Bree.

She shook her head. "Let him go. He's a total pain. He must have learned it from you."

Ha-ha. I was in no mood for Bree's sarcasm.

I spun away from Bree and ran down the hall. My sneakers thudded against the hard marble floor. I cupped my hands around my mouth and shouted my brother's name.

It didn't take long to find him. He had climbed the statue of Wonder Bat and was hiding behind the wings.

"Get off that!" I cried. "This isn't a playground. It's a museum."

"So?"

I made a grab for him, but he scrambled away. "You're going to fall off and break your neck," I said.

"So?"

I grabbed his ankles. He tried to squirm onto Wonder Bat's head. But I tugged hard, and he came toppling to the floor. "Stay off the statues," I snapped. "They're very valuable."

"So?"

I pulled him up from the floor. He tried to bite my hand, but I was too quick for him. Nice kid, huh?

Bree hurried over to us. She had her backpack on her shoulders. "Are we staying here?" she demanded. "If the museum is closed —"

"I wanted to show you everything they have," I said. "But something very weird is going on."

"Then let's leave. We can do our project at the Flower Museum. That's my favorite."

"The *what*? Did you say Flower Museum?"

She didn't answer. She was staring straight ahead. Her green eyes bulged in shock.

I turned and saw the big man bouncing toward us. I recognized his insane costume instantly. He wore silvery armor over blue-and-green tights and a leopard-skin cape. His tall white boots were covered in yellow feathers. His head was tossed back as he ran, and he let out a shrill, high-pitched giggle.

Dr. Maniac!

I froze and stared with my mouth hanging open. *How can this be? It's impossible! Dr. Maniac is a comic book character.*

Ernie jabbed me in the side with his elbow. "Who's the freak?" he whispered.

"Shut up," I whispered back. "It's Dr. Maniac. He — he —"

"Where am I?" Maniac cried. "What's happening?"

He stopped a few feet in front of us and gazed all around. He ran his hand through his wild, unbrushed red hair. The leopard-skin cape fluttered behind him. "Where am I? Is this Cincinnati? How did I get to Cincinnati?"

"This isn't Cincinnati," I said.

He blinked. He squinted at the three of us. "Who are you?"

Before we could answer, his eyes landed on me. "AHA!" he screamed at the top of his lungs. "THERE you are! My ARCHENEMY!"

His eyes narrowed. His face filled with menace. He moved toward me.

"No!" I cried. "I — I'm not your enemy. I'm Richard Dreezer."

"Your disguise is good," Maniac said. "But you can't fool me. You call yourself Richard Dreezer now? I don't care. Prepare to be torn to pieces!"

I gulped. "Huh? Torn to pieces? You're crazy!"

Maniac thumped a fist on the hard armor over his chest. "I'm not crazy!" he bellowed. "I'm a MANIAC!"

He grabbed me around the throat with a gloved hand and lifted me off the floor.

"No. No — please!" I begged. "Put me down. What are you going to *do*?"

"Say good-bye to your friends," Maniac shouted. He raised me high above his head. "Your story is over. Look up. You're about to meet CAPTAIN CEILING!"

I uttered a choked gasp as he heaved me with all his might.

I stared straight up as I sailed headfirst to the high ceiling. Then I shut my eyes and waited for the crushing pain.

12

Whoa. No crash.

No pain.

I opened my eyes when I realized I hadn't smashed into the ceiling. I felt strong arms around my waist. I turned my head and saw Dr. Maniac holding me.

We were inches from the ceiling, floating high above Bree and Ernie. His cape billowed around us. "Sorry," he murmured.

He sailed down and set me gently on the floor. My knees folded. I nearly fell. The room spun. My heart was pounding in my chest.

Dr. Maniac landed beside me. "Sorry," he repeated. "My mistake."

I swallowed. "Mistake?"

"You're not my archenemy — *are* you?!"

"No," I said, starting to feel a little more normal. "I told you — I'm Richard Dreezer. That's my brother, Ernie. And she's my friend Bree."

"Don't say friend," Bree said. "We're in the same class at school. That doesn't mean we're friends."

Dr. Maniac studied us. He had one blue eye and one brown eye. They rolled crazily in his head. He scratched his hair again.

"I'm very confused," he said. "All these statues and displays and comic book covers... Where *am* I?"

"Whoa. I'm confused, too," I said. "I mean, you're not real! You're a comic book character."

He gasped. "Huh? I'm not real? Are you kidding me?"

He raised a gloved hand and pinched his cheek. "Ouch. Hey, if I'm not real, how come I just pinched myself and it hurt?"

I shrugged. "Beats me."

He grabbed the top of my head. "Let's see if I'm real enough to spin your head like a top."

"No — please!" I backed out of his grasp.

"Hey, wait. Here's a good test," Maniac said. He bent and scooped up something in one glove. He raised it to me. A fat brown cockroach.

He shoved it to my mouth. "Go ahead. Eat this," he said. "Eat it. Let's see if it's real."

"Yuck. No way." I tried to back up and stumbled over Ernie.

"Eat it," Dr. Maniac insisted. He pushed the disgusting bug toward my mouth.

Ernie laughed. "Go ahead. Eat the cockroach, Richard. Eat it! Eat it!"

"Shut up," I told him. "Just be quiet."

"Oh, forget the whole thing," Maniac said. He popped the cockroach into his mouth. Bug juice squirted from his lips. "Mmm. Not bad. Kind of crunchy. Tastes like chicken."

Ernie laughed at him. "You're crazy!"

Maniac swallowed the cockroach. "I'm not crazy. I'm a MANIAC!" He tossed back his head and laughed.

Bree leaned forward and whispered in my ear. "This museum project isn't working out. Maybe Mrs. Callus will change her mind and let me work alone."

Before I could answer her, I heard a loud SQUISH. Then wet sucking sounds. THWUCK THWUCK THWUCK.

I turned to the front and saw another comic book character. He was squirming out from under the welcome desk. The big dude crawled across the floor on his hands and knees. He was covered from head to foot in thick mucus. And he moved in a wide, sticky puddle of goo.

Slugmaster Slime!

Dr. Maniac stepped in front of us as we watched the evil Slugmaster inch his way to the museum doors. He moved slowly, leaving a wet trail behind him.

"You're disgusting!" Dr. Maniac shouted at him. "Someone should step on you!"

"Come over here and try it." Slugmaster's voice came from deep in his throat. It sounded drippy and hoarse, like he had a really bad cold.

"I'd step on you and put you out of your misery," Maniac shouted. "But I don't want to get my boots sticky."

"Come over here and I'll slime your face!" Slugmaster croaked.

I watched in shock as the sticky supervillain crawled along his trail of mucus. He slowly disappeared out the door.

"He isn't real, either," I told Dr. Maniac. "None of this is happening. Maybe I'm having a nightmare."

"Well, let me *out* of your dream!" Bree cried. She started to the door — but stopped when another character rose up from behind the front desk.

He was big, broad shouldered. His head was huge and his face was as red as a tomato. His muscles bulged in his costume — purple tights and top, purple cape, purple helmet over his eyes.

I recognized him at once. The Purple Rage.

He leaped out from behind the desk. His face turned a darker red when he saw the three of us. *"Know what BITES my BABOON?"* he boomed. "YOU do! Outta my way!"

He started to the door — then stopped. He

stared at Dr. Maniac. His face formed an angry scowl. "Know what GRIPES my GRITS? Seeing YOU here!"

Maniac motioned with both hands for the Rage to back away. "Control yourself, Rage!" he cried.

"Control myself?" Rage screamed. *"Control myself?"* His face was as purple as his costume now. His eyes bulged, and his big chest heaved in and out. "Control myself? When someone says that to me, it puts me in a RAGE!"

He let out a fierce roar — raised both arms and leaped at Dr. Maniac.

"Hey — !" I let out a shout as Dr. Maniac ducked behind me.

And the Rage came sailing into me. His arms wrapped around my waist and tackled me to the floor.

"OWWW!" I hit the floor hard. My head bounced a few times. I actually saw stars.

Rage jumped to his feet and stuck his purple face in mine. "So you're working with that Maniac? Okay, kid. You asked for it. I'm angry now. You've steamed my oven mitts! I'm going to turn *him* into Maniac Meat. But first I'll destroy YOU!"

He raised a huge, purple-gloved fist. "Go ahead, kid. Count to three."

I gasped. "Huh? Count to three? Why?"

"It'll give you something to do while I pulp you like a wood chipper!"

13

Breathing hard, the Purple Rage waved his fist in my face.

"Uh ... could I count to *one hundred*?" I choked out.

He growled like an angry wolf. "Know what CRAMPS my KIPPERS? Jokes. I *hate* jokes when I'm about to shred someone like a dry sponge. It makes me AAAAANNNNNNN-GGGGRRRRRY!"

He pulled his huge fist back and —

And —

End of the Richard Dreezer story?

No. To my shock, Bree reached up and grabbed the big purple dude's arm. She wrapped her hands around his bicep and held his arm back.

"Listen to me, Purple Whoever-You-Are. Richard isn't working with that maniac!" she cried. "We don't know what's going on here. We're not comic book characters. We're just *kids*."

"I HATE kids!" the Rage muttered. He clamped his jaw shut and gritted his teeth.

"We're just kids who came here to do a museum project," Bree explained, holding on to his arm with all her might. "And now we want to leave."

Rage squinted at her. "Leave? Know what BOTHERS my BOBBLEHEAD? People who want to leave!"

Dr. Maniac stepped up to the Purple Rage. "Here's a riddle for you," he said.

Rage broke free of Bree's grasp and turned furiously on Maniac. "A riddle? Are you *crazy*?"

"I'm not crazy. I'm a MANIAC!"

Rage tossed back his purple cape. He brought his face up close to Maniac's. "Do you really think a riddle will keep me from cracking you like an overripe walnut?"

Maniac giggled. "What's red, white, and blue, and likes to pound supervillains like you to dust?"

Rage rubbed his chin. "Hmmm. That's a good one," he said. "I give up. What's red, white, and blue, and likes to pound supervillains like me into dust?"

Maniac giggled again. "It's the Star-Spangled BANGER!" he said. "And guess what? He's standing right behind you!"

"Huh?" The Purple Rage spun around.

Maniac wasn't joking. A powerful looking superhero, wearing the stars and stripes and a very ugly scowl under his red, white, and blue mask, rose up in front of Rage.

Without a word, the two of them began to fight. Grunting and growling, they threw each other to the floor. *WHOMP. WHOMP. WHOMMMP.* They punched each other furiously with gloved fists. And wrestled, rolling over and over.

I breathed a sigh of relief as they reached the door, still punching and clawing at each other. I waited for them to vanish outside.

But halfway out the door, the Purple Rage turned back and pumped a fist at me. "I'll be back for you, punk!" he shouted angrily. "And I'll flatten you like yesterday's wet laundry!"

Punk? Me?

Groaning and shouting, they began to wrestle again. And rolled right out of the museum.

I stood staring at the doors for a long time, my whole body trembling. I wanted to make sure they were really gone.

Then I turned to Dr. Maniac. "Wh-what's going on?" I stammered. "Tell me. What's happening here?"

Maniac kept his gaze on the museum doors. "I think I know," he said. When he finally turned to Bree, Ernie, and me, his face was solemn. "Sorry to tell you this. But I think it's a pretty big deal. I think it's the end of the world."

14

I let out a sharp cry. Bree's mouth dropped open. I could see she was breathing hard. Ernie scratched his head, his face twisted in confusion.

"It's the end of the comic book world as we know it," Maniac said softly.

"Excuse me?" I cried. "The *comic book* world?"

Bree frowned at him. "What are you talking about?"

Dr. Maniac's eyes flashed. "I have another riddle for you," he said. "What's the difference between an angry bumblebee and Christmas morning?"

Bree rolled her eyes. "Can we skip the riddles? Can you just tell us what you mean?"

"Give up?" Maniac said.

"Yes, we give up," Bree replied.

Maniac grinned. "I don't know the answer, either. But it's a pretty good riddle — isn't it?"

"Please," I begged. "Tell us what's happening here."

He swept his leopard-skin cape behind him. "There was always a wall between the comic book world and the real world," he said. "But do you see what has happened? Someone has opened the door between the two worlds. And the comic book characters are escaping into the real world."

I swallowed. "You mean like you, and the Purple Rage, and the Star-Spangled Banger?"

Maniac nodded. "Yes. We're all out in the real world now." He shook his head. "This could be a total disaster, kid. There's *no way* comic characters can fit in. No way we can get along with real people. There will be fights on every street corner. It will be WAR!"

I gasped.

"Uh . . . can I go home now?" Bree said. "I'm not really into comic books. This is kind of boring."

I turned to her. "Bree, you heard what he just said. Don't you want to save the world?"

"Not really," she answered. "I have a lot of homework." She tugged at a thick strand of her blond hair. "Also, I really don't want people to see me hanging out with you, Richard. You understand, right?"

Ernie burst out laughing. "Because he's a jerk?"

I gave Ernie a hard shove. Dr. Maniac stepped between us. "Forget about going home," he said. "I can't let any of you leave."

Bree scowled at him. "What do you mean?"

"I need you three kids to bring the comic book characters back to the museum."

"Us?" Bree cried. "You're crazy."

"I'm not crazy. I'm a MANIAC!" he exclaimed. He tossed back his head and laughed up at the ceiling.

Bree took off, running to the front doors. But Maniac flew across the hall, swooped in front of her, and blocked her way. She dodged left, then right. But he stayed with her.

"You can't keep us here!" she cried.

"Yes, I can," Maniac insisted. "You're my hostages now."

A stab of fear made me gasp. "Hostages?"

"That's my brilliant plan," he said. He grinned, thinking about his own brilliance. "It's going to work. I know it will."

"What's your plan?" I asked, my voice cracking.

"Simple," Maniac replied. "I'm holding you three as hostages, see. I'm going to tie you to chairs. Then I'm setting up TV cameras. Then I'm going to torture you with live tarantulas until you scream in agony."

15

"Th-that's your plan?" I stuttered. My heart was thudding in my chest. I glanced down at Ernie. His eyes were wide with fear.

"We have to get away from this nutcase," Bree whispered in my ear. "How can we get out of here?"

Dr. Maniac grinned at me. "That's my plan. Brilliant, huh? Especially the tarantulas part."

"But — but — how does that help with the escaped comic book characters?" I asked.

"Simple as pineapple upside-down cake," he said. "The comic book characters see you three kids screaming in pain from tarantula bites — and they come rushing back here to rescue you."

I stared hard at him. "And then?"

"Then I send them back to Comic Book World," he replied.

"Huh?" Bree uttered. "You call that a plan? That's insane."

"Of course it's insane," Maniac replied. "I'm a MANIAC!"

He forced us over to three folding chairs by the wall. Then he pulled out long black cords. "Don't just stand there. Sit down so I can tie you to the chairs," he said. "Then I have to go find me some hungry tarantulas."

I opened my mouth in a loud, explosive sneeze. "I have bad allergies," I told Maniac.

He squinted at me. "So?"

"So . . . I'm allergic to being tortured by tarantulas."

"I have to go home now," Bree said. "You can have your little comic book war without me. Seriously."

Ernie looked up at Maniac. "Torture Richard first — okay?" he said. "Not me. Richard really wants to go first."

Nice kid, right? I told you. He's a peach.

I sneezed again. My brain was spinning. I was trying to come up with a way to escape from Dr. Maniac. I pictured my body covered in tarantulas. Snapping tarantulas crawling all over me, dozens of them, snapping and clawing and biting while people all over the world watched on TV.

My whole body itched and throbbed. I could feel the intense pain already.

I had to do something. But *what*?

Maniac was already strapping Ernie's hands behind the chair.

Think of something . . . anything!

"Dr. Maniac, are you ticklish?" I asked.

He was leaning over Ernie, wrapping the cord around his hands. "Me? Ticklish? Yes, I am. Why?"

I dove to the floor. I grabbed one of Dr. Maniac's boots and quickly pulled a bunch of yellow feathers off it. Then I jumped to my feet and began to tickle him under the chin.

Maniac started to giggle. He tried to squirm away, but I kept the feathers under his chin.

He giggled some more. His giggles turned to wild laughter.

He stood helplessly as I tickled him harder. Faster.

The dude was incredibly ticklish. While he laughed and squirmed, Ernie ripped the cords off his hands. He and Bree raced to the front doors.

"Stop! Stop! Oooooheeey! Oooohey!" Maniac laughed like a maniac. Tears rolled down his face. He laughed till he couldn't breathe. He laughed till he choked.

Then he toppled onto his back, giggling and snorting. His arms and legs thrashed in the air, like he was a big turtle that had fallen over.

That's how we left him. Laughing at the top of his lungs, flopping like a fish on the floor. Totally helpless.

I followed Bree and Ernie out the door. I didn't look back.

We ran down the steps. The sun was nearly down. A cold evening breeze gusted at us. I could see a pale half-moon in the sky.

I couldn't wait to get home. I knew Mom and Dad would be worried about Ernie and me.

"We could take the bus to your house," Bree said.

"Let's just *run*," I said. "I don't want to wait for a bus."

We darted across the street and started to run along the sidewalk side by side. We only made it half a block.

Then we stopped — and gasped in shock.

"I — I don't believe it!" I cried. "This is *too horrible!*"

16

Across the street, two red-caped superheroes were fistfighting on the roof of the bank. The bank alarm blared. The doors shot open — and two other masked characters ran out, carrying big bags of cash.

A gigantic dude with red lobster claws instead of hands slapped his claws against the window of a jewelry store. The glass shattered. The claws frantically grabbed up the jewels in the window.

People screamed. A group of frightened teenagers ran down the center of the street. Cars crashed. Sirens cut the air.

Two costumed characters battled on top of a black SUV, trading punches while the driver screamed at them from down below. A brown-fur-covered supervillain as big as a rhino grabbed a screaming woman's purse and bounded off with it. Two hawklike characters with wide bird wings flapped into the air and took off after the enormous thief.

The frightened screams. The sirens. The THUD of fists as costumed characters pounded one another. The pounding footsteps as ordinary people tried to run from the scene . . .

It was all too much.

I covered my ears as I watched in horror. Dr. Maniac was right. It was definitely a war. The real world was being taken over by battling, robbing, screaming, out-of-control comic book characters.

Bree huddled beside me, her hands pressed to the sides of her face. "I *knew* we should have gone to a different museum," she said. "What a mistake."

"Huh?" I gaped at her. "We didn't cause this. Just because we were there doesn't mean —"

I ducked as a bald-headed, silver-costumed character flew low over our heads. I recognized him — the Bullet.

"This is cool!" Ernie declared. "Like being in a video game."

"But it's *real*," I said. "And it's dangerous."

"Look OUT!" Bree shrieked.

Two characters wearing tiger masks and yellow-and-black capes leaped off a building and crashed to the ground right behind us. I heard their bones crack as they hit. But they climbed to their feet and continued punching each other.

"We're *out* of here!" I cried. I dodged around the two battling tiger-dudes, lowered my head, and started to run.

The three of us ran without stopping until we reached my house. We passed two store robberies, an explosion, and several fistfights. A car squealed to a stop, and with a deafening crash, three cars piled into the back of it. The drivers burst from their cars and started punching one another.

Strange shadows swept over us as we ran, the shadows of comic book characters flying low in the sky.

I ran up the driveway to the back of the house. I pulled open the kitchen door and darted inside. Ernie and Bree followed closely behind. Did my parents have any idea what was going on out there?

"Mom! Dad!" I shouted. "Where are you? Mom! Dad!"

The kitchen was dark and empty. No food on the stove. The table hadn't been set for dinner.

"Mom? Dad?"

I ran through the hall, into the living room. And stopped with a startled cry. "Oh, nooooo!"

Ernie couldn't stop himself and banged into me. Bree stepped up beside me, her eyes wide with horror.

The two characters I'd seen on the way to school that morning — Captain Croaker and Terry Tadpole — slouched in their green costumes on our living room chairs. And Mom and Dad —

Oh, wow. Mom and Dad —

My parents were in cages. Metal dog crates. They were down on their hands and knees, crammed into cages against the wall.

"Mom! Dad! Are you okay?" I cried.

Inside her cage, Mom lifted her head. "We wouldn't be in this mess if it wasn't for your father," she said.

"My fault? How is it *my* fault?" Dad demanded.

"You opened the front door and let them in," Mom replied.

"I did not!" Dad said. "They hopped in through the window. If you hadn't left the window open, maybe we'd be okay."

Mom banged her cage bars with her fist. "Shut up, Barry. Can you just shut up?"

I couldn't believe it. Locked in cages — and they were still arguing!

I turned to the two froggy villains. "What are you *doing* here?" I shouted. "Let my parents *out!*"

Captain Croaker raised his feet to the ottoman and settled deeper into the chair. He patted the chair arms. He took his time answering me.

Finally, he croaked, "Don't make waves, kid. This is *our* lily pad now."

17

Terry Tadpole jumped to his feet. "You got a problem with that?" he growled in a deep, raspy voice. He stood straight up on the chair cushion. He was only about a foot tall.

"You — you don't belong here!" I stammered. My voice cracked. My heart had jumped to my throat. I felt like I couldn't breathe. "Let my parents out. You can't DO this!"

Bree gave me a shove and started to back out of the room. "I'm out of here," she said. "I have to see if my parents are okay."

Captain Croaker let out a long, deep croak. "Mmmmeeeep. You're not going anywhere, babe."

He opened his wide mouth — and lashed out a long, slender pink tongue.

The tongue flew across the room. It made a SLAAAP sound as it hit Bree.

Bree screamed as the tongue wrapped around her waist. She struggled to pry it off her. But the tongue wrapped tighter around her and started to pull her toward Croaker.

"Let go of me!" she screamed. "This is *sick*. Ohh, this is sick. Let me go!" She tugged frantically at the tongue with both hands.

Croaker's eyes flashed with excitement. He had a big grin on his green face. He pulled his tongue in, pulling Bree close, tightening it . . . tightening it.

"Can't . . . breathe . . ." she gasped. She turned to me, her face red, twisted in horror. "Richard . . . can't breathe . . . help . . ."

"Let her go!" I shouted. I tugged at the disgusting tongue. But it was coiled too tight. I couldn't loosen it.

Terry Tadpole laughed an ugly laugh. It sounded more like vomiting than laughing. "Come over here, jerk," he growled. "And I'll spit tadpole juice in your eye."

My brain was doing flip-flops in my head. I knew I had to act — fast. Bree was gasping and choking. Bouncing up and down on the chair, Croaker tightened his tongue around her waist.

Suddenly, I had an idea. A crazy idea. But maybe . . . Maybe . . .

I turned to Ernie. "Quick — go upstairs," I said. "Get your collection. You know. The collection in the glass jar. The one Mom thinks is so adorable."

69

Ernie blinked. It took him a few seconds. Then he understood what I was talking about. He spun around and raced to the stairs.

"Come back, squirt!" Terry Tadpole yelled. "Come back here and I'll squash you like a bug!" The ten-inch-tall supervillain opened his mouth and spewed a thick brown liquid into the air.

"He's ruining my chair," Mom said from down in her cage. "Look. He stained the cushion."

"Who cares about the cushion?" Dad said from the cage beside her. "Let us out of here!" he yelled at Terry Tadpole.

"Shut your yap," Terry Tadpole growled. "We keep our pets in cages. Get used to it, Fat Face."

"Fat Face?" Dad muttered something under his breath. Then he slumped silently in his cage.

I stared at Terry Tadpole, my whole body trembling. He was the toughest tadpole in comic book history. And now here he was in my house, and we were his prisoners, under his control.

And his fat-frog partner was choking Bree with his powerful elastic tongue. Her face was bright red. She made horrible gagging sounds. Her knees started to fold. Captain Croaker let out deep frog laughs, enjoying her fear.

I heard Ernie thudding down the stairs. Would my plan work?

Ernie burst into the living room, holding the glass jar in both hands. The jar contained his dead fly collection. Hundreds of dead flies.

Yes, my brother is deeply weird. But maybe . . . just maybe his collection would save Bree.

I took the jar from him and started toward Captain Croaker.

Everyone knows that frogs *love* to eat flies — right? So I thought maybe he'd go after the flies and unwrap his tongue from Bree.

I strode across the room. I held the jar out to the ugly green creature. "Dinnertime!" I cried. "How about it, Croaker? Looks yummy? How about some dinner?"

Please . . . go for it. Please . . . let go of Bree and start chomping down on the flies.

Croaker watched me approach. He raised his wet froggy eyes to the jar in my hand.

"How about it?" I asked, waving the jar in front of him. "Dinnertime?"

"No thanks," Croaker said. "I already ate."

18

"Huh?" I stopped a few feet in front of him. "You sure?"

He didn't answer my question. I stood there with the jar of dead flies raised above my head.

And then I sneezed. A powerful explosion. I sneezed again — and the glass jar dropped from my hand.

I jumped back as the jar hit the carpet. It bounced once. The dead flies came spilling out. The flies spread over the floor.

Terry Tadpole took a dive off the armchair cushion. He landed hard on the floor, grabbed a dry dead fly, and shoved it into his mouth with both hands.

"Leave it! Leave it!" Captain Croaker shouted.

I stared at him. How did he manage to talk with his tongue wrapped around Bree?

"Don't touch those," he screamed. "I told you, we're vegetarians now. You know meat makes us burp."

"But I like *meat!*" the terrible Tadpole cried. He shoved another fly into his mouth and chewed it hungrily. CRUNCH, CRUNCH.

"I said *leave it!*" Croaker bellowed angrily. "You're the sidekick. You're supposed to follow my orders."

Terry Tadpole ignored him and grabbed another dead fly.

Croaker let out a groan. He slid his tongue off Bree's waist, swung it through the air, and began to slap Terry Tadpole with it. "Leave it! Leave it!"

Bree staggered back, holding her waist, her face still red.

I grabbed her by the shoulders. "Come on — hurry!" I urged.

"Don't go!" Dad yelled. "You have to help us!"

But this was our only chance to get away. I pushed Bree into the hall. I didn't have to tell Ernie to follow. We shot through the kitchen and out the back door.

"We have to find help," I said, breathing hard. I glanced behind us as we ran to the street. The two villains weren't coming after us. "We'll need help to get Mom and Dad out of those cages."

"Maybe my parents can help," Bree said. Her blond hair flew behind her as she raced to the corner.

"Wh-what are those green guys going to do to Mom and Dad?" Ernie asked. He sounded frightened for the first time.

"They said Mom and Dad are their pets," I answered. "They said they keep their pets in cages."

"But —" Ernie started, then stopped. I could see the little guy was thinking hard. I think it finally dawned on him that this was really happening. The whole world had changed. All the scary stuff was *real*.

"My parents will know how to help," Bree said. "Dad is a firefighter, you know. He helps people every day. He'll know how to —" She stopped with a gasp.

It was nearly dark. The streetlights hadn't come on yet. The pale half-moon sent down shimmery light.

We stared up at her house. It was a square redbrick house. It stood behind a white picket fence on a low hill.

Something was on the front lawn. Something big and dark. Something tilting from side to side as it moved toward us.

In the dim evening light, I struggled to see what it was. And then I let out a cry as it came into focus, and I recognized it.

A huge brown beetlelike insect creature, as big as a school bus. Its antennae bent from side to side, then stood straight up as it lumbered on its prickly legs toward us.

Spiky black hair poked from the big bug's body. It snapped its jaws loudly and made a frightening clicking sound. It moved stiffly, like a giant insect robot.

And I recognized it from its comic book series.

"This is bad," I murmured to Bree and Ernie, watching it approach. "This is very bad."

"Who is it?" Ernie whispered.

"It's Halley Tosis."

"Huh?" Ernie stepped up close beside me. "Halley Tosis?"

"Also known as *Baaaad Breath*!" I cried.

And as I shouted those words, the ugly bug creature opened its mouth wide — and sent a thundering blast of putrid air flying toward us.

"Cover your nose!" I screamed. "Hold your breath! Cover your nose!"

Too late.

The sick odor poured over me. I breathed it in. I felt my stomach lurch.

Ohhhh, sick. It smells so rotten.

I started to gag.

Another blast of sour wind from deep in the insect's belly — and all three of us dropped to our knees, gagging and choking.

I couldn't help it. My stomach heaved and I started to retch. I bent over and vomited noisily into the grass.

Bree was bent beside me, gagging, pressing her fingers to her nose. She waited for me to stop heaving up my lunch. Then she muttered, "I'm never doing a project with you again."

"Ullllp." Ernie made a gagging sound. He held his throat. "I . . . can't breathe . . ." the little guy moaned. "The smell . . . it's so bad. It's sticking to my clothes. Help me, Richard. It's sticking to my *skin*."

"Whooooah." I started to puke again.

When I finally looked up, I saw a sight that made my whole body shudder. Another comic book character came striding down the lawn toward us. I recognized him instantly.

The Purple Rage. He was back!

He knocked Halley Tosis down and stomped toward us at the fence, head lowered, fists tight at his sides.

The Rage looked angry.

"We're doomed," I muttered. "We're totally doomed."

19

"Know what BLOWS my BLUBBER?" the Rage boomed, swinging his fists as he came at us. "Everything!"

Even in the pale moonlight, I could see that his face was as purple as his costume. His boots sank into the grass as he strode across the lawn.

The three of us huddled together, unable to move. Behind the Rage, I saw Halley Tosis struggle to his spindly insect feet.

Down the street I heard an explosion. Police cars rocketed by, their sirens blaring.

The Bad Breath Bug lumbered up behind the Purple Rage — and let go a powerful *whoosh* of putrid air.

The Rage doesn't stand a chance against that sick smell, I thought.

But I was wrong.

The purple villain swung around — and grabbed a section of the white picket fence. With a roar from deep in his chest, he hoisted it from the ground and raised it in front of him like a shield.

The blast of smelly air hit the fence — and bounced back over Halley Tosis. The big bug made an ULLLLP sound. His front legs shot straight out. As the smelly air rolled over him, his antennae drooped, then fell limp over his head.

His whole body slumped. He gasped for air, choking and sputtering. He shut his eyes, and his head dropped forward.

I let out a cry as he toppled onto his back in the grass. And didn't move.

Killed. Killed by his own smell.

Bree, Ernie, and I didn't have time to celebrate. The Purple Rage ripped away another section of the white picket fence and strode up to us. "Know what SKINS my SOUPSPOON?" he boomed. "Kids who smell like *skunks*."

He pressed his fingers over his nose. "You *reek*!" he cried. "Get away from me! Get away from me — now!"

He was right. The three of us smelled *horrible* from the big bug's breath. "But we need your help!" I cried.

He let out a roar. "Helping people makes me *angry*."

"Get over yourself!" Bree shouted. "We're in trouble. And our parents are in trouble."

The Rage stared at her through his purple mask. "Know what POPS my PINEAPPLE?

Parents who get in trouble." He shook his fists in the air. "I can't take all this trouble!"

He tilted back his head and started to roar. He swung his fists high above his head. "I'm in a RAAAAAAAGE!" he bellowed.

He twirled around, faster and faster, until his cape was tangled around him. Then he stopped, took a deep breath — and came hurtling toward us.

"No — please!" I cried, my voice tight with panic. "Please! Don't hurt us!"

20

I dodged to the side. I couldn't stop myself. I bumped Bree hard, and the two of us fell to the grass.

The Purple Rage burst past us and kept running. Roaring out his furious rage, he flew across the street and crashed headfirst into a fat tree trunk.

KLONNNNK. It sounded like wood smashing into wood. The ground shook. My breath caught in my chest.

The Rage fell to his knees. A few seconds later, he climbed back to his feet. "There. That's better," he said calmly.

He shook himself like a dog after a bath. Shook his whole body. Then he came walking slowly back to us. "I feel like a new man."

We heard screams down the block. Another explosion in the distance. More sirens.

"Wh-what are we going to do?" I stammered.

"I know who is behind all this craziness," the Rage said, smoothing down his cape. "I know who started this. I know."

We gazed at him silently, waiting for him to tell us.

"I can tell you whose fault it is in two words," the Rage said. "Just two words."

"What two words?" Bree asked.

"*Maniac*," he replied.

"But . . . *Maniac* is only *one* word," I said.

"See? That's just how dangerous he is!" the Rage exclaimed. "What happened to the other word?"

"This guy is a maniac, too," Bree whispered in my ear. "I'll never forgive you for this, Richard." She stomped really hard on my foot. Ernie hooted with laughter.

"Huh? Me?" The whole world was in trouble, and she was blaming *me*!

The Rage rubbed his chin. "Dr. Maniac opened the door between the comic book world and the real world," he said. "Dr. Maniac let everyone escape."

"But . . . why?" I asked.

"Because he's a MANIAC!" the Rage cried. He thumped his chest with a fist and screamed at the sky for a while.

"I know why he did it," he said finally. "To make me angry." He stomped toward the street.

"Come on. We're going back to that museum. We're going to force Dr. Maniac to make things right again."

"But — but — it's night," I sputtered. "The museum will be closed." I knew that was a lame excuse, but it was the only thing I could think of.

"I have a special key to the door," the Rage said. "See this?" He raised his big fist. "This is my key."

He stomped rapidly along the sidewalk, his cape ruffling behind him. "This really WRECKS my ROOSTER!" he cried. He uttered an angry roar — and *punched* a low tree limb.

I saw something go flying across the street. It took me a few seconds to realize what had just happened.

"Bree," I whispered. "He . . . he just punched a *squirrel*! He's so insane, he just punched a squirrel off a tree. Do you really think we should follow him?"

"What choice do we have?" she snapped. "Your parents are in cages. And I don't know where my parents are. Look at my house." She pointed behind us. "It's totally dark. We have no choice, Richard. We have to find a way to turn things back the way they were."

And that's how we ended up back at the Comic Book Museum for the most terrifying night of our lives.

21

A few minutes later, we followed the Rage up the concrete steps to the museum entrance. The lights were on and the front doors were wide open.

I knew what that meant. It meant that more comic book characters were escaping their world and running out into our world.

We burst into the front entryway and gazed all around. No one in sight.

"Know what PICKLES my PASTA?" Rage boomed. "Everything!"

I took a few steps into the front hall. *Where is Dr. Maniac?* I wondered. *Did he fly off into our world, too? How will we ever find him?*

The Purple Rage adjusted his purple tights as we walked down the long hall. "I hate when they crawl up on me," he muttered. He turned to me. "I come from the Angry Planet. Everyone stays angry all the time. Have you read my origin? It's one of the top-rated origin comics on everyone's list."

"Yes. I've read it," I said. We passed the statue of the Unknown Superhero. I kept my eyes straight ahead, searching for any sign of Dr. Maniac.

Bree stayed close behind us. I knew she was really worried about her parents. Her face was pale, her expression grim. She didn't bother to fix her hair. She didn't say a word.

"What's *your* origin story?" the Rage asked me.

"Huh? Me?" The question startled me. "Uh . . . My origin? I was born. That's all."

The Rage snickered. "We could call you Captain Boring."

We were nearly to the end of the hall. I peered into the auditorium. Dark and empty.

Bree was squinting into one of the display rooms. She turned, shaking her head sadly. "There's no one here," she said in a trembling voice. "We're wasting our time."

The Rage let out an angry growl. "Know what CRINKLES my CUCAMONGA? Finding an empty museum. I know that maniac is here somewhere." He shook a fist in the air. "If we find him . . ."

I heard a shrill scream. From the front of the museum.

"Hey — Ernie?" I cried. I spun around. "Where's Ernie?"

Another high scream. It definitely sounded like my brother.

"Is that him?" Bree said. "Did he wander off again?"

We went racing back to the front. Our shoes slapped the marble floors as we ran.

"Ernie? Ernie?" I shouted his name over and over.

And his cry came back: "Help me! He's taking me away! Help me! Hurry!"

I skidded to a stop as the front desk came into view. "Noooo!" I screamed.

I saw Ernie and Dr. Maniac behind the desk. Maniac held Ernie in both hands, high above his head. Ernie kicked and squirmed and thrashed, but Maniac held him tightly.

"Help meeeee!" Ernie screamed.

Struggling to fight off my panic, I screamed, "Let him go!"

Then I took a deep breath — and hurtled to the front desk.

Too late.

They both vanished.

22

"Ernie? Where are you? Can you hear me?"

Of course he couldn't hear me. He was gone.

I leaned over the desk and searched behind it. No one there.

My poor brother. He sounded so frightened. I shuddered. I suddenly felt frightened, too. I gripped the desk with both hands.

I was in charge of Ernie. I was supposed to take care of him . . . watch out for him. And I let him down.

Still trembling, I turned back to Bree and the Purple Rage. "Why?" I cried. "Why did Maniac want Ernie?"

The Rage squinted at me. "Because he's a MANIAC?"

Bree ran up beside me and searched behind the desk. "But . . . where are they?" she asked. "Where did they go?"

The Rage let out a shout. "Know what BANGS my BAZOOKA? When villains like Maniac get

86

away!" With a loud roar, he ran full speed across the room and *kicked* the wall.

"Owwwwww!" The pain made him howl. He hopped up and down on one foot. Finally, he walked back to Bree and me. "I have to stop kicking things," he said. "But what else can you do when you're angry? I tried punching myself in the head. But that didn't feel good, either."

"What do we do now?" I asked. "I have to get my brother back."

He placed a gloved hand on my shoulder. "Follow me, Richard."

I blinked. "Follow you? Where?"

"Into Comic Book World," he said. "You want your brother back, right? We have no choice. We have to go there to find him."

"But — but —" I sputtered.

"How do we get there?" Bree asked. "Look around. I don't see any door with a sign marked *This Way to Comic Book World.*"

I turned to the Rage. "You came through the door. Tell us where it is."

He scratched his forehead. "I know it's right here somewhere," he said. "But where? I was so angry, I forgot to look. Doesn't that PUNCH your PETUNIA?"

I had a flash. "The wastebasket," I said.

They both stared at me. "What about the wastebasket?" Bree asked.

"There were two comic book characters," I

said. "Standing behind the desk. They were both standing in the wastebasket."

The Rage clapped his purple gloves together. Then he slapped me a high five. "Yes. I remember now!" he said. "They were coming up from the other world — through the wastebasket. Just like me. Good work, Richard."

But then his expression changed. His face darkened. "Know what PUNCTURES my PECCADILLO? It makes me angry that I didn't remember that!"

"Never mind," I said. "Let's go. Ernie may be in big trouble. We don't want to waste another second."

My heart pounding, I swung myself around to the back of the desk. Bree and the Rage scrambled after me.

"Quick — into the wastebasket!" the Rage cried.

"Hey, wait —" I uttered. "I don't believe it!"

The wastebasket was gone.

23

"It — it can't be," I stuttered. "It was always right here."

"AAAAARRRRRGGGGH!" The Rage bellowed a furious cry. "That totally BOGGLES my BABUSHKA!"

He roared again, swinging his fists over his head in a total rage.

With a swing of his boot, he kicked the whole desk over. It crashed onto its side.

And as he danced around in pain, I stared at the floor. At the shiny black metal handle poking up in front of me. I bent down and grabbed the handle with both hands. I tugged it up.

A trapdoor. A trapdoor that had been hidden under the desk.

"Hey — look!" I shouted.

The Rage leaned over me. "Yes! That's it," he said. "Now I really remember. That's the passageway."

I gazed down into the opening. I saw only total blackness.

A wave of panic chilled my entire body. *I don't want to go down there. If I do, will I ever get back?* The frightening thoughts made my head spin.

But I knew I had no choice. I had to find Ernie.

I turned to Bree. "Are you coming?" I asked.

She shrugged. "If we go down there, maybe we'll get extra credit for our museum project."

I dropped onto my knees and started to lower myself into the opening. Bree tapped me on the shoulder. "But I really don't want to be seen with you in the other world, either," she said. "You understand, right?"

"Right," I said. I didn't really care. I only cared about rescuing my brother.

I turned and lowered my legs into the darkness of the hole. My feet found a ladder on the side of the opening. I stepped onto a rung and waited for my heart to stop racing. Then I lowered my feet to the next rung.

"Climb down and wait for me." I heard the Rage call. He seemed very far above me as I took the next rung down. Then the next.

I couldn't see a thing. Darkness covered me like a blanket.

I gripped the sides of the ladder with both hands. My hands felt slippery and wet. I peered down, hoping to see some light or the ground.

90

But I saw only solid black without a glimmer. So dark I couldn't tell if my eyes were open or closed.

"Take your time, Richard. Easy does it." The Rage's voice seemed very far away now. Almost in another world.

I took one more step and — whoooooah!

My foot hit air. Only air. No ladder rung.

Both feet dangled now. I struggled to find a place for them to land. But — no.

Oh, no.

My hands slipped off the sides. I fell free from the ladder.

Too frightened to let out a cry, I fell through the thick blackness.

How far would I fall? How long before I hit?

The air whooshed up around me as my body dropped down the passageway.

I finally screamed as I splashed into icy water. My scream cut off as I sank, sank into the bottomless black water.

24

I thought I'd sink forever. *Swim!* I told myself. *Move! Do something! You're going to drown.*

My chest already felt about to burst. I thrashed my arms hard, and I struggled to kick my legs.

My clothes clung to my skin. I felt as if my shoes weighed four hundred pounds. But I forced myself to swim. Stroking hard, I pulled myself up . . . up toward the surface.

The darkness lifted. The water filled with an olive-green light. I needed to get to the surface. I needed to breathe.

I pulled myself up . . . up . . . and finally my head rose above the bobbing green water. I sucked in breath after breath, raising my eyes to a charcoal-gray sky.

I was still breathing hard when I saw an enormous tentacle rise up from the water. It was dark brown, covered with pulsing pink suction pods.

The creature raised a second tentacle and began to glide toward me. And then I gasped in horror as I realized there were *two* giant bulgy-eyed creatures moving to attack.

Two enormous squids splashed up on a wave in front of me. Their tentacles were like tree branches. They waved them toward me, as if reaching for me. Their fat bodies pulsed and . . . and . . .

And . . . I recognized them from their comic book. Squeezer and Squisher, the Squid Twins. The Squid Twins who always squeezed their enemies to death and then battled each other to see which squid would swallow them whole.

ULLLLLP.

Panic swept over me. But I knew I had only seconds. I forced my brain to *work*.

From reading their comic, I remembered how to avoid them. I froze. I tightened every muscle. And let my body slide down into the water. I imagined that I was a log, a solid, heavy, sinking log.

Holding my breath, I tried not to move a muscle. I let myself drop. I kept my eyes on their giant, dark bodies and ugly, curling tentacles. And waited . . . waited . . .

Sure enough, they swam right over me. Their giant shadows rolled over me, darkening the water. They bobbed with the water, moving slowly, heavily. It seemed to take hours. But finally, they floated out of sight.

I pushed myself back up to the surface. I

raised my head to the sky and took several breaths. Air never tasted so good!

Blinking away the salty water, I pushed my wet hair out of my eyes.

I shielded my eyes with one hand and searched for land. There *had* to be land somewhere nearby. Those superheroes and villains didn't all live in the water.

The waves rocked me back and forth as I squinted into the distance. I spun all the way around. The water gleamed and sparkled like gold, making it even harder to see.

"Yes!" I uttered a cry when an island came into view. I saw a narrow stretch of white beach. Close enough to swim to.

I can do it. I can make it over there.

I took a deep breath, lowered my head into the water, and began to swim. The waves rocked against me, as if trying to push me back.

I kept a steady pace, raising my head to breathe, but my arms and legs began to ache. My head throbbed.

Closer. Closer . . .

I can make it. I know I can.

As the island grew nearer, I stared at the white shore.

What a strange island. No trees. No vines or bushes of any kind. It gleamed under the sky like a white rock.

I'm almost there. I can almost touch it.

94

The waves rose higher, rocking me back. But I lowered my head into the foaming water and pulled myself . . . harder . . . harder.

I stretched out both arms, grabbing for the land. Grabbing for the safety of the island.

And uttered a high scream of horror when the island opened a gaping mouth. And I saw rows of jagged teeth the size of tombstones. And it whipped around, revealing a giant black eye as big as a basketball.

And I knew instantly . . . knew it wasn't an island, after all.

It was a white whale as BIG as an island!

Comic Book World was such a dangerous, horrifying place. What made me think I could just swim to safety here?

That was my last thought as the gigantic jaws opened wider, and the waves washed me inside . . . past the pointed teeth . . . over the slippery warm tongue . . .

I shoved out both hands and tried to stop my slide. But the fat tongue flicked me back. I toppled onto my back and, in a rush of water, fell into the creature's vast belly, dark and icy.

25

I came to a stop against the spongy stomach wall. Small fish swirled and splashed around my feet along with tangles of slimy seaweed.

Shivering, my whole body shuddering, I hugged myself. The whale's belly made loud gurgling sounds. More water washed in, carrying dozens of fish into the darkness.

I gagged. The whale's belly smelled of dead, rotting fish.

Doomed, I realized. *I'm whale food.*

And then I heard a shout.

"This RIPS my RUTABAGA! This RUFFLES my ROTUNDA!"

The Purple Rage. His voice boomed and echoed through the dark whale belly.

In the dim, flickering light, I saw him and Bree. They leaned against one side of the pulsing stomach wall. Seaweed washed and tangled around them.

Bree shook a fist at me. "When will I forgive you for this? Try never."

"Wh-what are we going to do?" I stammered in a tiny voice. "What *can* we do?"

"We're . . . trapped," Bree said softly. "Trapped. Until we're . . . digested."

The Rage opened his mouth in an angry roar that shook the whole whale belly.

He shut his eyes. He squeezed his face, tightening it like a fist. The Purple Rage went into a furious *rage*. He screamed. He bleated like a goat. He roared like a lion.

And then . . . and then . . .

The Rage EXPLODED.

Like a powerful bomb blast. His body flew apart. Pieces of it flew everywhere. The blast roared and shook the whale belly.

A tidal wave rose and swept forward. And I felt myself being lifted out of the belly . . . sliding along the smooth tongue. . . . Yes, the explosion blasted me out of the whale, sent me flying high on top of the cresting wave.

"Ohh!" I was hit by a blinding light. The sun!

I sailed high . . . high and far. I landed hard on my back on solid ground. A beach. A real beach.

I hit so hard the breath whooshed out of me. Choking, gasping, I struggled to breathe.

When I looked up, I saw Bree lying on her back on the beach. From here, I couldn't see her face clearly, but I could see her blond hair. She was digging her elbows in the sand, struggling to sit up.

Was she okay?

"Bree!" I shouted. My voice came out hoarse and high. "Bree!"

"Richard!" she cried. "My leg — it's *broken.* Oh, it hurts. It hurts. My leg! Ohhh, help!"

My lungs still aching, I pulled myself to my feet. I brushed sand off my clothes. I started to run to Bree. But I stopped with a horrified cry.

Bree's leg . . .

. . . her leg . . .

I held my breath and struggled to fight down my horror and panic.

Bree's leg had come off. It sat a few feet away, in the sand, like a piece of driftwood. All by itself.

26

"Help me, Richard. My leg! My leg!"

I spun away and shut my eyes. I couldn't stand
to see the leg lying there. But even with my eyes
closed, I couldn't erase the horrifying picture.

What can I do? How can I help her?

She was screaming and beating the sand with
her fists. Was she in horrible pain?

I turned back. And a thought flashed through
my brain.

*We're not in the real world. We're in Comic
Book World now.*

The rules are different. Anything can happen.

Maybe.

I took a deep breath and forced myself to walk
over to the leg. My shoes squished in the wet
sand. My clothes were soaked and smelly from
the inside of the whale.

I carefully lifted Bree's leg with both hands.
Her white sneaker was still attached to the foot.
I brushed sand off it. I carried it over to Bree.

"What are you doing?" she screamed. "What do you think you're doing?"

"Calm down," I said. "I'm trying something."

I bent down and shoved the leg back into place. I held on to the shoe, pushing the leg hard for a moment. Then I let go. "Try to move it."

Bree kicked her leg. She raised it into the air, then lowered it. It was attached again! Amazing.

With a groan, she climbed to her feet. She didn't thank me. Instead, she gave me a hard shove. "If we survive this, I'm going to *kill* you," she said.

"I'm sorry," I said. "But it's kind of exciting being in a whole new world, isn't it?"

"No," she said. She kicked sand on my legs.

"Well, I have to find Ernie," I said. "My brother is here somewhere, and —"

That's when I saw the footprints. Small footprints in the sand, leading toward the trees at the edge of the beach.

"Those could be Ernie's," I said. "Let's follow them."

"Whatever," she muttered.

Following the trail of footprints, we started off the beach. But Bree was limping badly. She groaned with each footstep.

"Now my *other* leg hurts," she moaned. "Hope it doesn't fall off, too. I definitely need a doctor."

"Do you want to wait here until I find one?" I asked.

"No way," she said. "We're not splitting up in this creepy place." She turned and led the way, limping along the path through the trees.

We walked through a jungle of tangled trees and vines. I didn't hear any birds. I didn't see any other creatures.

"How are you going to get Ernie away from that maniac?" Bree asked. She brushed a dead leaf from her hair.

"Easy," I said. "We can tickle him and make him helpless like we did before."

She rolled her eyes. "I don't think it'll be that easy."

Sunlight spilled over us. The trees gave way to a flat, open field of tall grass. We followed the narrow dirt path through the grass.

Bree was limping badly. I could see she was biting her lower lip to keep from crying out in pain.

"Look. There's a town up ahead," I said, pointing. "Maybe we can find a doctor there."

"Do you think Mrs. Callus will give us extra credit on our project for coming here?" Bree asked. "I mean, if we survive."

"I don't want to think about that," I said. "I just want to find my brother."

We walked through the town. Past a large bank, a supermarket, a bookstore. All empty.

The whole town was deserted. No one anywhere. Nothing moving. No cars. No dogs. No super-heroes flying overhead.

Bree stopped and leaned against the front of a bakery window. "How come we're the only ones here?" she said. "This is seriously freaking me out."

"I guess they all escaped through the trap-door," I said. "They all left Comic Book World and went to the real world."

"Why were they so eager to get away?" she asked.

I shrugged. "Beats me. This looks like a nice town."

But Bree was right. The silence was frighten-ing. The empty streets . . . the empty stores . . . all terrifying. Wasn't *anyone* left in Comic Book World?

"Hey, check it out," Bree said. She limped across the street and I followed her.

We stood in front of a low white building. The windows were covered by dark window blinds. But a sign at the front door revealed that the building was a doctors' office: TWO DOCTORS — NO WAITING.

I gripped the door handle. "Do you think they're still here?" I asked Bree. "Or did the doctors leave with everyone else?"

"Only one way to find out," she said. She shoved me out of the way and pulled open the door.

I stepped in after her. We were in a brightly lit waiting room. I saw a row of black chairs, a table piled high with magazines, a bubbling fish tank on one wall.

And then I turned to the front desk — and let out a cry of surprise.

27

The woman behind the desk wore a red costume. Her face was half-hidden under a red mask. Her red cape was draped behind her chair.

Of course I recognized her. The Scarlet Starlet.

In her comic book series, she was a Hollywood star. When she wasn't in front of the cameras, she was a superhero. What was she doing in this doctor's office? Was she playing a part in some movie?

I gazed around. No movie cameras.

She glanced up from the papers on her desk. "Can I help you? Do you have an appointment?"

"No," I said. "We just —"

"The doctor is very busy," she said. "If you don't have an appointment, scram." She motioned to the door.

"But there's no one else here!" I said.

"And I think my leg might be broken," Bree chimed in.

The Scarlet Starlet squinted at Bree. "Interesting. The doctor has never treated a broken leg before. You'd be the first."

Bree's eyes went wide. "The doctor doesn't treat legs?"

"He doesn't treat patients," Starlet replied. "Sick people make him nervous. He only sees people who have no problems."

"That's crazy," Bree said. "What kind of a doctor doesn't treat sick people?"

"He's a very good doctor," the Starlet said. "He just isn't interested in your health. He —"

She stopped. A shrill scream from the back office interrupted her. The door was closed. But I heard the scream clearly. And then more shouts, sounds of a scuffle, and another scream.

"What's going on back there?" I asked.

The Starlet didn't answer. She stood up and walked to the office door. She pulled it open, then turned back to us. "Dr. Maniac will see you now," she said.

Huh? Dr. Maniac?

Yes. He stood grinning at us in front of an examination table. Dr. Maniac, wearing a white lab coat under his leopard-skin cape, with a stethoscope around his neck.

"You — you're not a real doctor," I blurted out.

"I'm not a doctor — I'm a MANIAC!" he cried.

Bree narrowed her eyes at him. "What were those screams we heard?"

"That was me," Maniac said. "Just doing my morning exercises."

He took a deep breath, then let out a long, high scream. Panting, he took the stethoscope and listened to his own chest. "Hey, I'm not breathing!" he cried. "Somebody call a doctor!"

"*You're* the doctor," Starlet said from the doorway. "Go to the phone and call yourself."

"But today is my day off!" Maniac cried.

I'd had enough of his comedy act. I stepped up close to him, my hands balled into fists. "Where is my brother?" I demanded. "We saw you take him. What have you done to him?"

"Your brother?" Dr. Maniac shook his head. His expression turned serious. "I'm soooo sorry," he said in a whisper. "Your brother didn't make it. Squeezer and Squisher, the Squid Twins, got him. It . . . it was very messy."

28

A stab of horror made me gasp. "That's not true!" I screamed.

Maniac nodded. "You're right. It's not true. I lied." He shook his head. "It's such a bad habit. Why do I lie all the time? Is it because I had an unhappy childhood?"

"I don't care," I said, my voice trembling. "I just want to see my brother. Where is he? *Where?*"

Maniac rubbed his chin. "Come to think of it, I had a very *happy* childhood. So why am I such a terrible liar? Is it because I'm a maniac?"

"I don't care!" I screamed again. I picked up the stethoscope from the front of his lab coat and shouted into it, "Where is my brother?"

Maniac shrieked and jerked the stethoscope from his ears. "Ouch. I'm deaf now. I'm totally deaf. Call a doctor!"

"You're a doctor," the Scarlet Starlet called from the front room.

"But I can't see myself!" he cried. "I don't have an appointment."

I raised my fists. I was about to lose it. "Ernie!" I shouted. "Are you here somewhere? Ernie? Can you hear me?"

I heard a bang. A hard thud. The door to the supply cabinet against the wall burst open. And Ernie came toppling out.

He landed on his side and quickly scrambled to his feet.

"You're here!" I cried happily. "You're okay!"

He rolled his eyes. "What took you so long?"

"Give us a break," Bree said. "We had to leave the real world behind to come here and rescue you."

"Well, get me out of here!" Ernie shouted.

"Not so fast," Dr. Maniac said, stepping to block the door. "I think you'll learn to like it here."

"Like it here?" Bree cried. "Seriously?"

"We're going home," I said. I took Ernie's hand and started to pull him out of the office.

Dr. Maniac spread his arms to keep us back. "Richard, I knew if I brought your brother here, you would come down to rescue him. And now I have all three of you as my guests. My guests — forever."

"Guests? You mean *prisoners*?" I asked. My heart started to pound in my chest.

"That's such a harsh word," Maniac said. "Why

don't we say *friends*. You are my new best friends. And best friends stick together, right?"

"I don't want to be your friend," Ernie said. "I want to go home. Why don't you keep Richard? He's really into comic books. Why don't you keep him and let me go home?"

Nice kid, huh?

Glad I risked my life to save him.

Dr. Maniac's smile faded. His voice turned cold. "Forget about going home," he growled. "*This* is your home now. Deal with it."

29

"Why?" I cried. "Why do you want to keep the three of us here?"

"Don't worry," he said. "There will be more of you. There will be hundreds of you."

Bree plopped down on the chair behind the desk. "This isn't happening," she murmured to herself. "I know this isn't happening." She tore at her blond hair with both hands.

"Everyone left Comic Book World," Maniac said. "All of my comic book friends. They all escaped to the real world. I need people *here*. I need people to live in *this* world."

"You're a maniac!" I cried.

He smiled. "So what else is new?"

"But — but we can't —" I sputtered.

"Listen to me," he said. "Comic book characters all want to live in the real world. So I'm going to bring *real people* to live in Comic Book World."

"But you can't do that to us. We don't belong here!" I cried.

He raised a gloved hand to silence me. "Real people," he repeated. "Real people. Real people to obey my every command. Real people to be my slaves." He giggled. "Won't that be fun?"

"No way!" Ernie cried. He dove across the room and tried to kick Maniac in the leg.

But the supervillain dodged to the side, and Ernie ran headfirst into his cape.

Shouting angrily, Ernie got all tangled, and Maniac had to pull him out.

"Don't you realize how lucky you are?" Maniac asked. "People never age in comic books. That means you'll stay young for the rest of your lives!"

"We — we'll be kids forever?" I stammered.

"Oh, thrills," Bree muttered.

I edged over to where she was sitting. I leaned forward to whisper to her. "If we all make a run for it at once, he won't be able to stop us."

She turned and stared at the door. "Maybe . . ." she whispered back.

But Maniac must have overheard us. Or maybe he was a mind reader. Because he swung quickly to the office door — and clicked the lock.

"Okay, slaves," he said. He clapped his hands together. "Let's talk about all the wonderful things you're going to do for me."

111

"I'm hungry," Ernie said. "It's dinnertime back home. What do you have to eat?"

Dr. Maniac narrowed his eyes at him. "You're joking, right? There's no real food in Comic Book World. Comic characters don't eat real food."

"We're going to *starve*?" Ernie cried.

Maniac never had a chance to answer.

A deafening roar shook the room. I was slammed against the wall as a sharp blast shattered the windows.

I ducked. Jagged shards of glass flew across the office.

A shadow fell over us as someone leaped onto the window ledge. He jumped into the room, his purple cape flying behind him. His boots crunched the glass shards beneath him.

The Purple Rage!

He took a few steps toward Maniac, hands on the waist of his purple tights, his biceps bulging. Then he saw Ernie, Bree, and me.

"How can you be here? You — you exploded!" I cried.

"I pulled myself together," he said.

"Get us out of here!" Ernie said.

"Thank goodness you're here," I said. "You can free us from this maniac."

The Rage stared hard at me. "You're kidding, right? Help you? Did you forget I'm a villain?" He put his arm around Maniac's shoulders. "I'm on *his* side now."

30

Maniac and the Rage both laughed evil laughs. They bumped knuckles and laughed some more.

Bree sat behind the desk, shaking her head sadly. Ernie had a droopy look on his face. He shoved his hands deep in his pockets and lowered his head.

I have to admit I felt pretty defeated, too. This was definitely looking bad for us.

I had my eyes on the locked office door. My brain spun. I tried frantically to think of a way to escape.

I thought of the Scarlet Starlet. She was seated at the desk on the other side of the door. If I called her, would she open the door and let us out?

No way.

I gazed at the smashed window. It was wide open now. Could the three of us get to the window before Maniac and the Rage hauled us back?

No way.

"Know what PINCHES my PIGGYBANK?" the Purple Rage boomed. "Everything!" He pulled back his fist and with a powerful swing, punched it into the wall.

His fist cracked the plaster and shot deep into the wall. The Rage let out a howl of pain.

"Why did I just do that?" he cried.

"Because you're a maniac?" Dr. Maniac suggested.

"No," the Rage growled, pulling his fist from the wall. "Sometimes I just get so angry, I want to punch my fist into a wall."

He turned to me. "You ever punch your fist through a wall just because you felt like it?"

"No," I said. "Never."

"You should try it," he said. "Now that you're in *our* world, you should try to develop some bad habits, kid."

"I'll try," I said.

And that made an idea flash into my head.

Yes. Yes. Ernie, Bree, and I weren't in our own world. We were in *their* world. The superhero supervillain comic book world.

So . . . maybe that meant I had superpowers, too.

Anything is possible here — right?

I mean, Bree's leg was halfway down the beach. And I fixed it just by pushing it back on.

So I could have superpowers in this world. Powers I can use to get the three of us out of here.

Maniac and the Rage weren't expecting me to try anything. I had surprise on my side.

I tried to signal to Bree and Ernie that I was about to try something. But they were both staring down glumly at the floor.

Quickly, I made a plan. I decided to tackle Dr. Maniac, send him tumbling into the Purple Rage. Then get the others moving — and fly out the window.

Could we fly? Why not? This was Comic Book World. *Of course* we could fly.

My chest felt all fluttery. My hands were ice cold. Sure, I was nervous. But I knew I could do it. I knew I could be a superhero and help us escape.

I took a deep breath, leaped high — and dove across the room at Dr. Maniac.

31

"OWWWWW."

A cry burst from my throat as I fell flat on my face.

I hit the floor hard, knocking my breath out. Pain shot through my whole body.

I don't have any superpowers.

Gasping for breath, I shut my eyes and listened to the two supervillains laugh.

Oh, wow. They thought it was a riot. They tossed their heads back and hee-hawed at the top of their lungs. They slapped each other on the back and laughed some more.

And I realized this was our chance.

I pulled myself to my feet. Then I gave Bree and Ernie a shove toward the door.

Maniac and the Rage were still laughing and high-fiving each other. I tore across the room and pulled open the office door.

The three of us darted past the Scarlet

Starlet. She looked up, surprised. "Leaving so soon?" she said.

"We're out of here!" I cried breathlessly. My heart pounding, I led the way toward the front door.

But another huge figure in a white lab coat stepped in front of us. "Not so fast," he growled.

I gasped in shock. I recognized him at once.

"Dr. Root!" I cried. "The allergy doctor! What are *you* doing here?"

32

The huge man lumbered toward us. His round pink face glowed in the bright office lights. He kept his arms outstretched, ready to stop us if we tried to run around him.

"Stay calm, Richard," he said. "Everyone stay calm. You're perfectly okay."

"But — but —" I sputtered. I couldn't believe he was here. He didn't belong in this world.

"Who *is* he?" Ernie whispered.

"My new allergy doctor," I whispered. "He gave me a shot that didn't work and —"

"Yes, I gave you a shot," Dr. Root said. "And you fainted. Do you remember that part, Richard?"

I pictured that two-foot-long needle, and my whole body shuddered.

"Yes, I remember that," I said.

"Well, let me explain things to you," Root said. "This is all a dream."

"Huh? Excuse me? A dream?"

"Don't you see?" he said. "You fainted from the shot, and you're having a nightmare. That's all it is."

Bree gave me a hard shove in the side. "A nightmare? Why do I have to be in your nightmare?"

"I . . . don't get this at all," I said.

When I turned back to Dr. Root, he had another hypodermic needle in his hand. Another *two-foot-long needle*!

"Wh-what are you going to do?" I stammered, taking a step back.

His tiny black eyes narrowed at me. "I'm going to give you another shot to wake you up. After this shot, you'll be just fine. Trust me."

Trust him? Why should I trust him?

He raised his blubbery arm and thundered toward me.

In a total panic, I turned to Bree. "Quick — pinch me!" I cried.

Bree squinted at me. "Did you say *pinch* you?"

"Yes. Hurry. Pinch me hard."

"I'd *love* to!" she said. She grabbed my arm and dug her fingers and thumb in as hard as she could.

"Owwwwww!" I opened my mouth in a shrill scream of pain.

I took an angry step toward Dr. Root. "You're a LIAR!" I shouted. "This is definitely not a dream."

"Okay, okay," he said. He lowered the needle

to the side of his fat stomach. "I lied." He rubbed his flabby chins. "Want to know the truth?"

"Sure. The truth," I said, still angry. "How about it? How about telling us the truth."

"I'm the one who opened the passage between the two worlds," Root said. "I was the first one out. Didn't you wonder why my office was right across the street from the Comic Book Museum?"

"No," I said. "No. I didn't think . . ."

"Why did you do it?" Bree demanded. "Why did you open the door between the two worlds?"

His smile made the flab on his face quiver. "I knew if I could open the door," he said, "I could cause panic everywhere."

"But — *why*?" I cried. "Why did you want to create panic?"

He stuck out his chest proudly. "Because . . . I'm the *Root of All Evil*!" He tossed back his head and opened his mouth in an evil comic-book laugh. "Maniac and I — we're maniac partners! Maniacs forever!"

Then he raised the mile-long needle again. "Now stand still, Richard. This will only hurt for a second."

33

I tried to back up. Behind me, I saw Dr. Maniac and the Purple Rage watching from the door to the back office. They both moved forward to keep me from escaping Dr. Root.

"Leave him alone!" Bree screamed at the huge doctor. "Leave Richard alone!"

But his tiny black eyes locked onto me, and he raised the needle higher.

Panic made my legs buckle. I couldn't move. Couldn't breathe.

And then I *sneezed.*

I gasped in surprise as the sneeze blew the needle right out of Root's chubby hand.

The needle flew into the air, then fell and bounced on the carpet.

The big man bent down to grab it — and I sneezed again. A powerful jet blast of a sneeze.

It sent Dr. Root slamming backward into the wall. He hit so hard, the whole office shook. He sank to the floor like a dead whale and didn't move.

My sneezes are like explosions here, I realized. *Have I found my superpower?*

"This KICKS my KIELBASA!" the Purple Rage screamed. Roaring angrily, he lowered his head and came running at me.

I let out a super-sneeze and sent him flying backward across the room. He landed on his back on the desk. The Scarlet Starlet screamed and jumped to her feet.

Dr. Maniac opened his mouth in a crazy, high-pitched giggle. His eyes rolled in his head. He tossed back his cape and flew across the room, hands outstretched to grab me.

I sneezed so hard, I nearly knocked *myself* over. Maniac gasped as my sneeze blew his hair straight up in the air. I sneezed again and sent him crashing against the wall.

"Run!" I cried to Ernie and Bree. "Go! Go! I'll hold them here with my super-sneezes."

They both took off.

Shaking his head, Maniac pulled himself to his feet. He looked dazed. He turned angrily to the Scarlet Starlet. "Why aren't you helping us?" he cried.

She raised both hands and wiggled her fingers. "I'm waiting for my nails to dry."

"That's CRAZY!" he shrieked. "Don't you see we have a PROBLEM here?"

"Don't shout at me, Maniac," she replied coldly. "I'm a *star!*"

I turned and saw Ernie and Bree rocket out the door.

Dr. Root groaned. But he was still knocked out.

Maniac pulled the Rage to his feet. He dragged the Starlet beside him. The three of them were lining up, preparing an all-or-nothing attack.

Yes, I was outnumbered. But I had an awesome weapon.

I scratched my nose, making sure it was ready.

"Know what PIPS my PIPE?" the Rage screamed. "You actually think you can beat us."

Dr. Maniac giggled. "No way you can win, Richard. You're only a wimpy kid with bad allergies."

"Wrong," I said. "I'm a wimpy kid with super-sneeze powers!"

"He has a certain star quality," the Scarlet Starlet said. "He really should talk to my agent."

The Rage growled at her. "Shut up and attack him. Come on — let's go!"

I didn't give them a chance to move.

I sucked in a deep breath — and *sneezed* as hard as I could.

The mighty blast sent all three of them crashing into the wall. They hit hard and cracked right through the plaster, into the back office.

Wow! This is fun! Seriously!

I spun around and darted to the door. I pushed it open and ran outside. Into bright daylight.

Where are Bree and Ernie? I wondered. *Can we get back to the real world?*

Blinking in the sudden bright light, it took me a moment to see the crowd. The crazy crowd, running, flying, leaping around, fighting and shouting.

"Whoa! What is going on?" I shouted.

34

I stared up and down the crowded city block. My mouth dropped open in shock.

Superheroes fought on rooftops and sidewalks. Wildly-costumed men and women swung from ropes and slid along webs. Characters flew overhead, their shadows trailing under them on the street.

I heard deep frog croaks and saw Captain Croaker hopping in the park on the next block. He was followed closely by his little sidekick, Terry Tadpole.

"Look ouuuuuut!" a voice screeched.

I ducked as Ziggy and Higgy, the Battling Bat Brothers, zoomed right at my head. Whistling and screeching, they soared into the sky.

"Crime does not pay!" a voice boomed behind me.

"But it's a good hobby!" someone else shouted.

I turned to see two yellow-costumed superheroes with their longbows raised, firing flaming arrows at each other.

I realized I was holding my breath. I let it out in a long whoosh.

I blinked. Then I rubbed my eyes. *Am I imagining all this?*

"What *happened*?" I cried.

"We all came back," said a voice beside me. I turned to see the pulsing red face of the Caped Corpuscle. "We couldn't stand it out there."

"Huh?" I gasped. "You all came back? Why?"

His face pulsed and throbbed. Under his red costume, I could see the blood racing through his whole body.

"The real world is too boring," the Corpuscle said. "Too quiet. No fun at all. Why would anyone want to live in the real world? They don't let you fly or fight or do anything up there."

"Uh . . . I need to get back to the real world," I said.

He squinted at me. "Seriously?"

"Seriously," I said. "I think my brother and my friend have already returned. I don't see them anywhere. And now, I have to return to the real world, too."

"That's a shame," the Corpuscle said, shaking his bloodred head.

"A sh-shame?" I stammered. "Why is it a shame?"

"Because the door is closed. Closed forever."

35

My heart skipped a beat. "You mean . . . I'm *stuck* here?"

The Caped Corpuscle nodded. "Yes. The trapdoor is closed. Sealed tight."

"No, it isn't, you liar!" a gruff voice shouted.

It was the Mighty Hairball. He came bouncing up to us and bumped the Corpuscle off the sidewalk with his hairy brown chest.

"Get away from me, Hairball!" the Corpuscle warned. "I'll *bleed* on you. It won't be pretty."

"The trapdoor is still open a tiny bit," Hairball said to me. "But it's closing fast. You'd better hurry, kid." He pointed to a concrete stairway across the street. "Take those stairs. The trap door is at the top."

"But . . . but . . . where's the water? Where's the beach?" I stammered.

"This is Comic Book World," Hairball replied. "Things change all the time. Better hurry."

Corpuscle stepped up to Hairball. "You'll never forget the day you called *me* a liar!" he screamed. "My blood is *boiling* now!"

Hairball bounced onto him, knocking him over. Blood puddled all over the street. The two weird superheroes started to fight, wrestling, punch ing each other.

I took off, running to the stairs.

"Trapdoor, please be open," I murmured as I took the steps two at a time.

I climbed higher. And now I could see the trapdoor above me.

Yes! It was still open a bit. Open just enough for me to squeeze through.

"I'm coming!" I shouted. "I'm almost there!"

I reached a small landing. I stopped to catch my breath.

"I'm coming!" I shouted up to the trapdoor. I could see it slowly closing. I started running again.

And something big fell on me. Like a big sack of potatoes. It landed on my head and shoulders and drove me to the landing floor.

I groaned with pain and struggled to squirm out from under it.

A big, heavy, hairy body. It held me down. It sat on my chest. It wouldn't budge.

Over its hairy shoulder, I saw the trapdoor slowly closing.

The creature on top of me raised his face.

I stared at his mask. I knew it. I *knew* that mask.

The Masked Monkey!

"Let me go!" I cried.

I could see the trapdoor creaking shut overhead.

"Let go! Let go of me!"

36

The Monkey pressed his heavy body down on me. I couldn't move.

I knew I had only one chance. One way to defeat him.

I tried to take a deep breath. I opened my mouth wide, and tried to sneeze.

No. Not happening.

Come on. Come on! I needed a super-sneeze to blast the hulking creature off me.

I sucked in another breath. Opened my mouth. And —

No.

I groaned as the the big monkey leaned forward, pressing his paws over my shoulders. He pushed his chest into my face. The fur ... the thick fur tickled my nose. The fur made my whole face tingle.

I tilted my head back — and let go with a powerful explosion, a roaring sneeze.

I felt the Monkey's paws slide off me. I opened my mouth and sneezed again. The Monkey flew off me . . . staggered back . . . back to the edge of the platform.

Another sneeze. And the startled creature's mask blew off his face.

I saw his chimplike face for the first time. The whole face appeared to crumble. The Masked Monkey slumped in a heap to the concrete. He lowered his head and began to cry. Loud monkey sobs.

Without his mask, the Masked Monkey was a powerless wimp.

I felt like cheering. My superpowers had defeated a classic comic book character. But I knew I didn't have time to celebrate.

I whirled around and darted up the stairs. My shoes clomped heavily on the concrete. My chest felt about to burst.

I was halfway up the stairs when the shadow of the ceiling fell over me. I gazed up — and uttered a horrified cry.

The heavy THUD rang in my ears as the trapdoor slammed shut.

37

Trapped. Trapped in Comic Book World forever.

With a defeated sigh, I pulled myself to the top of the stairs. I stepped under the trapdoor and gazed up at it.

I raised my hands to the bottom of the door. The wood felt warm. I spread my hands out and pushed hard.

The trapdoor didn't budge.

I held my breath, tightened my muscles, and pushed harder.

No. I wasn't strong enough. I couldn't move it.

I stared up at it. The real world was so close — but so far away.

Something tickled my nose. A bit of monkey fur?

I sneezed so hard, I nearly fell down the stairs.

The trapdoor sprang open. It swung high, then slid back down. I held my breath as it stopped — before closing all the way. The opening was big enough for me to squeeze through.

"Whoa!" I let out a cry as I saw my parents up there. I brought my face close to the open trap-door. I could hear them.

"This is your fault, Barry," my mother shouted at my dad. "Why didn't you go down there and pull him up?"

"How could it be my fault?" Dad protested. "Why is everything always my fault?"

"Because it's always your fault?" Mom shouted back. "Because you're a total loser?"

"Sure, I'm a loser," Dad said. "I'm married to *you!*"

Didn't they see me down here? Couldn't they stop arguing for one minute, even when I was in major trouble?

And then I saw Bree. Yes! She had found the staircase, too! She was safe and sound up there. She gazed down into the opening of the trapdoor — and saw me.

She scowled at me and shook a fist above my head. "Don't worry," she said. "I'll find a way to pay you back for this, Richard. I'll get revenge."

And then my parents finally stopped arguing and spotted me.

They both bent down and reached out their hands to me. "There you are," Mom said. "You're in a lot of trouble."

"You're going to be grounded for *life*," Dad said.

"Hurry, Richard!" Mom cried. "The door — it's closing again. Hurry!"

Yes. The door was creaking shut. I reached up my hands to them. I started to climb out. The opening was just wide enough. I could slide through easily.

But then I stopped.

I pulled back my hands. I gazed up at the closing door.

My heart was thumping. I could feel the blood pulsing at my temples.

I'd made a big decision.

Can you guess what I decided?

38

"So long, everyone!" I shouted. "Have a nice life!"

I watched the trapdoor slam shut.

Then I let out a cry of joy. "Yes! Yesssss!" I pumped my fists above my head.

I leaped off the stairs. I felt so happy I could explode. I darted past the Masked Monkey and flew down the rest of the stairs.

Comic Book World was so much fun. I knew I'd have a great life here. After all, I was a super-hero in Comic Book World — not a loser kid with allergies and a bad-news family.

I was CAPTAIN SNEEZE! Or should I call myself THE NOSE? Or maybe BLASTER? How about BLASTER MASTER?

I thought of name after name as I trotted down the street. All around me, comic charac-ters were fighting, flying, leaping after one another, having an *awesome* time.

"This is where I belong!" I shouted at the top of my lungs. "This is where I want to live!"

Then I saw the three costumed figures march-
ing down the street with their eyes trained on
me. Dr. Maniac, the Purple Rage, and Dr. Root.
They stood tensed, their bodies stiff, fists ready
for a fight.

"Come on!" I shouted. "Bring it on! Let's see
what you've got!"

I rubbed my nose, getting it ready for battle.
This is what I always had dreamed of.

I took off, running toward the three villains. But
after a few steps, I stopped short — and uttered a
cry of horror. "What are *you* doing here?" I cried.

Ernie hurried up to me, shaking his head.
"Guess I wandered away," he said. "I got lost. I
didn't find the stairs in time."

I gasped. "You mean —"

He kicked me hard in the leg. "I'm hungry," he
said. "Get me some food. And I'm tired. Where
are we going to sleep? Hurry up, Richard. I'm
really starving."

He kicked me again. "I need my game-player.
How can I get my game-player back? Where are
we going to live? I need a double cheeseburger.
Are you going to get me a double cheeseburger?"

Oh, wow. Oh, wow. Oh, wow.

I shut my eyes and pictured the trapdoor.
Closed tight. Closed forever.

My brother and I were trapped together.

*And just think, we're NEVER going to get a
day older.*

Goosebumps® MOST WANTED

The list continues with book #6

CREATURE TEACHER: THE FINAL EXAM

Here's a sneak peek!

My name is Tommy Farrelly. I'm twelve, and I wanted to hang around home with my friends this summer. But that's not happening.

My parents are forcing me to go to Winner Island Camp. What kind of camp is that? Well, let me tell you the camp slogan. It's: *Winners Are Always Winners.*

That's right. It's a camp where they teach you how to be a winner.

Now, I'm a totally normal guy. I'm happy most of the time. I do okay in school, mostly As and Bs. And I've got some good friends. So, I don't mean to brag or anything. But I think I'm *already* a winner.

But that isn't enough for my family. In my family, you have to be a **WINNER**. In my family, you have to be the fastest, or the luckiest, or the smartest, or the funniest, or the *best*, day and night.

My dad is a big, strong dude, about a mile wide. He played middle linebacker on his college football team, and they went to the national championship. Now he's a football coach at a junior college. All he cares about is *winning*.

My mom is a vice president at a bank. And she's into long-distance bike racing. Sometimes she gets up at four in the morning and rides for sixty miles before breakfast.

Even Darleen, my six-year-old sister, is a superstar. She was reading huge books when she was four. Last year, she won the National Spelling Bee in Washington, DC, against a bunch of high school kids.

Get the picture? I like to chill with my friends and take it easy. How did I get in this family?

And now, here we were pulling up to the dock. In about an hour, the boat was going to come to take me to Winner Island. I saw a little white restaurant near the end of the dock. Above the door, a wooden sign carved like a fish read: *Andy's Fish Shack*.

The lake sparkled blue and gold. The water rippled gently under bright sunlight. But my parents never take any time to enjoy a beautiful view.

We piled out of the car, and Dad cried, "Race you to the restaurant."

Mom, Dad, and Darleen took off, running as fast as they could. Their shoes slapped the wooden dock. I took one last look at the shimmery lake. Then I trotted after them.

Darleen reached the restaurant door first. "I call the window!" she shouted. She pulled the door open and disappeared inside.

"First one to the table gets the biggest breakfast," Dad said.

Do you see? Everything is a competition in my family.

Andy's Fish Shack was small with only a few tables. They had red-and-white checkered tablecloths. It was morning, but the restaurant smelled of chowder and fried fish.

A skinny old guy in a sailor's cap and a long white apron was wiping glasses behind the bar. I guessed he was Andy. "Take any table, folks," he called. The place was empty.

Darleen grabbed a seat by the window. I stopped to gaze at the long, silvery swordfish mounted over the bar.

"Last again, Tommy," Mom said, shaking her head.

Darleen giggled. "Tommy is always last."

"That's why we're sending him to Winner Island Camp," Dad said. "When he comes back in two weeks, you'd better watch out, Darleen. He'll beat you to the table every time."

She rolled her blue eyes. "No way." My sister has a round face and crinkly blond hair. My parents say she looks like a little doll.

That makes her a winner again since I'm kind of short and chubby, and I wear glasses.

The waiter took our breakfast order. Dad ordered three eggs and an extra helping of bacon to make sure he got the biggest breakfast. Mom competes by eating the *least*. "Could I just have the egg whites, please?" she asked. "And no potatoes."

Wind off the lake rattled the window by our table. Outside, I saw a seagull dive into the water.

I had a heavy feeling in the pit of my stomach. "I don't understand why I have to go to this camp," I said. "I mean, seriously."

"It's only two weeks, dummy," Darleen said.

"Don't call me dummy," I snapped.

Mom and Dad like it when Darleen and I fight. They say it shows we both want to win. It shows good competitive spirit.

My parents are weird — right?

"Your sister is right," Dad said. "The camp is only two weeks, but it's really going to toughen you up. You're going to come back a different kid."

Mom pulled the camp brochure from her bag. "Tommy, look what it says. This is Uncle Felix talking. He's the camp director."

She read from the brochure. "'When you arrive, you are a LOSER. But losers NEVER leave Winner Island.'"

Those words gave me a chill. I mean, what does that *mean* — losers never leave? Where do they go? What happens to them?

Guess what? I soon found out. And it wasn't pretty.

Andy set the breakfast plates on the table. Dad grinned. "I win. I got the biggest breakfast."

"But my eggs are the yellowest," Darleen said. It wasn't funny, but Mom and Dad both laughed.

"I don't *want* to be a different kid when I come back," I said. "I just want to be me."

Darleen gave me a hard shove. "Who would want to be *you*?" she said. Again, my parents laughed as if that was the funniest joke in the world.

"Hey, I see the boat!" Darleen pointed out the window. "I saw it first! I saw it first!"

I turned and saw a white boat, moving fast toward us, bouncing on the blue-green water.

The heavy feeling in my stomach was now a huge rock. "Dad, this isn't fair," I said. "I'm two days late to this camp. It already started. The other kids will have a total advantage over me."

He swallowed a mouthful of eggs. "That's good for you, Tommy," he said. He waved his fork at me. "You'll just have to be even tougher."

"Hey, I finished first!" Mom cried. She showed off her empty plate.

She usually wins the fast-eater prize.

Dad dropped some money on the table and we hurried outside.

Seagulls screeched and flapped above the little boat as it bobbed up to us. A young man appeared on the deck and leaned over to tie a thick rope around the post on the dock.

His long brown hair fluttered in the wind beneath a red baseball cap turned backwards. He had short brown stubble on his cheeks and wore ragged denim cutoffs and a red-and-blue camp T-shirt with the word *Winner* across the front.

He gave me a salute. "Are you Tommy?"

I nodded.

"Welcome aboard. I'm Jared. Jump on. Let's go to Winner Island."

A sharp wave made the boat bounce and tug at the rope.

My family gathered around me. Mom wiped a smudge of egg off my chin.

"Let's say good-bye to the *old* Tommy," Dad said. "Can't wait to see the *new* Tommy." He patted my shoulder. "Let's see who can hug him the hardest."

"No, please —" I started.

Too late. Darleen grabbed me around the waist. She tightened her arms around me with all her strength.

I heard a *craaaaack*. Pain shot up and down my body.

"My ribs!" I cried. "You *broke my ribs*!"

Groaning in pain, I hobbled onto the boat. Dad handed my duffel bag to Jared. He shoved it inside the cabin.

I gazed around, looking for other passengers. But of course, I was the only passenger. Camp started two days before. We were late because my parents insisted on competing in a barbecue championship in Santa Fe.

The little boat bobbed from side to side. Jared pointed me to a bench seat at the back. "I know it's a lake, but it gets a little rocky, dude," he said. "Don't throw up on the boat, okay? Only losers throw up on the boat."

"Okay," I said, dropping onto the bench. "No problem."

He disappeared around the cabin to the front. A few seconds later, the motor started up with a roar. The boat bobbed away from the dock.

I waved to my family. They waved back. I knew they were about to have their race to the car.

They vanished from view as the boat scooted over the lake. The late morning sun sent gold ripples on the gentle waves. The water sparkled all around me. Above the boat, chattering seagulls followed us for a while. Then they gave up and turned back toward land.

Hypnotized by the shimmering gold in the water, I just sat and stared for a long while. My family seldom takes boats anywhere. Mom and Dad say they are too slow. But I found it relaxing to bob on the gentle waves and smell the fresh air.

I saw a stack of camp brochures beside me. I picked one up. It snapped me out of my relaxed mood. I gazed at a photo of the camp director, Uncle Felix. He was bald and kind of mean-looking, with narrow slits for eyes. He had a red bandanna around his neck.

I read another quote from Uncle Felix:

At my camp, you won't just win, you'll win BIG-TIME. We EAT LOSERS for breakfast at Winner Island.

"Whoa," I muttered. I tossed the brochure to the floor.

"It's just another sports camp trying to sound different," I told myself. "And my parents totally fell for it."

I wondered if they had tennis. Tennis and swimming are my best sports. My parents started giving me tennis lessons when I was about as tall as the racket. I'm not a great player. But my forehand is as good as my backhand.

I pulled out my phone. I tried to text my friend Ramon back home. Then I saw that I had no bars. I remembered what the brochure said — no phone or Internet anywhere near Winner Island.

About the Author

R.L. Stine's books are read all over the world. So far, his books have sold more than 300 million copies, making him one of the most popular children's authors in history. Besides Goosebumps, R.L. Stine has written the teen series Fear Street and the funny series Rotten School, as well as the Mostly Ghostly series, The Nightmare Room series, and the two-book thriller *Dangerous Girls*. R.L. Stine lives in New York with his wife, Jane, and Minnie, his King Charles spaniel. You can learn more about him at www.RLStine.com.

NOW A MAJOR
MOTION PICTURE

JACK BLACK

Goosebumps

IN THEATERS
2015

THERE'S ALWAYS ROOM FOR ONE MORE SCREAM!

An all-new series from fright-master R.L. Stine!

The Original Bone-Chilling Series

—with Exclusive Author Interviews!

NIGHT of the LIVING DUMMY
R.L. STINE

DEEP TROUBLE
R.L. STINE

MONSTER BLOOD
R.L. STINE

the HAUNTED MASK
R.L. STINE

ONE DAY at HORRORLAND
R.L. STINE

the CURSE of the MUMMY'S TOMB
R.L. STINE

BE CAREFUL WHAT YOU WISH FOR
R.L. STINE

SAY CHEESE and DIE!
R.L. STINE

the HORROR at CAMP JELLYJAM
R.L. STINE

HOW I GOT MY SHRUNKEN HEAD
R.L. STINE

SCHOLASTIC

www.scholastic.com/goosebumps

GBCL22

R. L. Stine's Fright Fest!
Now with Splat Stats and More!

REVENGE OF THE LIVING DUMMY
R.L. STINE

CREEP FROM THE DEEP
R.L. STINE

MONSTER BLOOD FOR BREAKFAST!
R.L. STINE

THE SCREAM OF THE HAUNTED MASK
R.L. STINE

DR. MANIAC VS. ROBBY SCHWARTZ
R.L. STINE

WHO'S YOUR MUMMY?
R.L. STINE

MY FRIENDS CALL ME MONSTER
R.L. STINE

SAY CHEESE - AND DIE SCREAMING!
R.L. STINE

WELCOME TO CAMP SLITHER
R.L. STINE

THE SCARIEST PLACE ON EARTH!

HELP! WE HAVE STRANGE POWERS!
R.L. STINE

ESCAPE FROM HORRORLAND
R.L. STINE

THE STREETS OF PANIC PARK
R.L. STINE

WHEN THE GHOST DOG HOWLS
R.L. STINE

LITTLE SHOP OF HAMSTERS
R.L. STINE

HEADS, YOU LOSE!
R.L. STINE

WEIRDO HALLOWEEN
R.L. STINE

THE WIZARD OF OOZE
R.L. STINE

SLAPPY NEW YEAR!
R.L. STINE

THE HORROR AT CHILLER HOUSE
R.L. STINE

SCHOLASTIC

www.EnterHorrorLand.com

GBHL19B

Catch the MOST WANTED Goosebumps® villains UNDEAD OR ALIVE!